MOONLIGHT RISES

Text copyright © 2012 by Vincent Zandri
All rights reserved.
Printed in the United States of America.
No part of this book may be reproduced, or stored in a retrieval system, or transmitted in any form or by any means, electronic, mechanical, photocopying, recording, or otherwise, without express written permission of the publisher.

Published by Thomas & Mercer
P.O. Box 400818
Las Vegas, NV 89140

ISBN-13: 9781612183442
ISBN-10: 1612183441

MOONLIGHT RISES

A DICK MOONLIGHT THRILLER

VINCENT ZANDRI

f THOMAS & MERCER

For Laura

The eagle picks my eye
The worm he licks my bone
I feel so suicidal
Just like Dylan's Mr. Jones
Lonely wanna die
If I ain't dead already
Ooh girl you know the reason why.

—John Lennon

PROLOGUE

You're dead.

You're floating above a hospital bed that's served as your final resting place for the past twenty-four hours, ever since the cops dragged your sad body from out of that back alley.

You're dead.

Really stone dead this time.

You stare down at yourself and you're amazed at how fucked up you look. Like fifty miles of chewed-up road. White skin and bones, your now tight-jowled face carrying only a scarred remnant of its former baby-cheeked charm. "All teeth," as your mortician father used to say, cringing at the sorry state of some terminally ill neighbor (and, quite likely, his next client).

You have to admit it: maybe those cops shouldn't have rescued you at all. Maybe they should have just cut to the chase, left you for dead on the black, pee-soaked macadam. Because in the end, in the final analysis, all those tear-jerking, heroic attempts the Albany Medical Center staff made at resuscitation turned out to be all for nothing. Because now you're dead. And there isn't a single thing the doctors or God or Buddha can do about it.

There is, however, one bright light that shines against all that darkness:

Your girlfriend, Lola.

At least Lola has stood by your side through every second of your final struggle. At least Lola has been true blue. She's stood by your deathbed-side until the bitter end, just like any one of those famous, gladly-take-a-bullet-for-my-sig-other couples that have come and gone throughout history. Like Mary and Joseph, Antony and Cleopatra, Bonnie and Clyde. Like John and freaking Yoko.

And oh my, my, if she isn't looking choice today.

Long, velvety dark hair draping narrow shoulders. Tall, sexy body. Tight white Levi's over black cowboy boots. The Noconas you bought for her during a weekend getaway in N-Y-C. Black lace push-up bra under a loose, white, low-cut, V-neck T-shirt. She's got these white-rimmed Jackie Os covering sad brown eyes. Jackie Os that were designed to hide the never-ending tears of a cursed Kennedy wife. Makes you feel all sorts of warm and fuzzy inside even if your soul has left your body to become just an unidentifiable, immeasurable mass of transformed heat energy.

If only you could reach out, hold her one more time, tell her all those corny I've-seen-the-other-side-of-life things. Tell her you're going to a wonderful place, that death really isn't the end, that you'll wait for her, et cetera, et cetera. You want to wipe away her tears with a single index finger, just like Patrick and Demi in Ghost.

Lola, I'm so in love with you right now, more than I ever was in life. I'm so...

That is, until a strange man enters the hospital room.

Can't quite make out the dude's face since he's wearing a baseball hat and sunglasses, and you're forced to look down at him from up at the ceiling. But he's about your own height, Gold's Gym slim, wiry, no stranger to sweat-soaked workouts. And you should know. Up until this little life-ending mishap the most fun you had with your clothes on was bench-pressing two-thirty-five for ten reps.

Maybe you can't see his face, but you sense that he could be young. Like, real young. Like not-even-over-thirty. He's wearing a tight T-shirt, black leather jacket, tight blue jeans, and yeah, he's got some brand-new cowboy boots going too.

Noconas. Black.

Identical to the pair you own. Like he got his pair during a cozy afternoon shopping date to the mall followed by a major face-sucking session in the parking lot. At least, that's the way it had been for you not so long ago. You and Lola.

Dude comes so close to your girlfriend he's practically kissing her on the mouth, his left hand gently brushing up against her left butt cheek. Your car wreck of a body isn't even cold yet and this jerk is about to make out with your sig other right inside the room where, by the grace of God, your soul is leaving the building. Some precious-time-to-be-alone-with-your-dearly-departed-loved-one this turned out to be.

You get like, what, one of these look-at-your-own-dead-body deals in a lifetime? And now the sig other has to go and ruin it for you.

But then, hold on a second. Take a deep breath. You've got an idea. What if you try to make like a skydiver and dive right back into your body? You've heard about those dead people who've come back to life just like that when they've appeared to be gone-baby-gone. What if you try to dive back down into your body so you can jump the hell out of that bed, put those bench presses to work, and kick Gold's Gym's scrawny ass for good?

But as much as you wish re-entry, you know there ain't no goin' back for the dead-and-almost-buried. There's only the sad sight of your former girlfriend walking out of the hospital room, her brand-new, buffed-out Some Young Guy floating close behind and no doubt admiring her choice posterior. And damn if he never did even have the decency to show his face. As if he knew all the time that you were watching him.

So what to do?
Catch your breath and start over.
This time with the basics.

Here's the deal: you're dead.

Some gang of three big-ass mofos wearing President Obama Halloween masks and pressing handheld electronic synthesizers up against their necks to mask their voices, pulled you off the street, dragged you into a back alley, beat you with fists, boot heels, and pistol barrels, and left you to bleed out alone. They said almost nothing to you, except for the tall barrel-chested one in the middle, who spat, "You should have stayed away from Peter Czech!"

You couldn't figure out if the voice was foreign or not. Not with that synthesizer pressed up against his voice box. Anyway, that's when you blacked out.

And now that you're dead, you can see that your girlfriend has been doing the wild thing behind your back with someone else. Name and face not known. Maybe for a short time, maybe for a long time. You have no idea. All you know is that he's a stud man and she's probably giving him a hummer right now inside her four-wheel-drive, gas-guzzling Hummer in the AMC parking garage.

But you know what? You're no longer angry or jealous.

Maybe that's because of the speck of bright white light forming in front of your eyes. You begin to feel yourself moving from the ceiling toward the light, through this tunnel at lightning speed. It's like something out of the Discovery Channel. You're moving faster than light itself. You're not afraid of the speed, not afraid of crashing, not afraid of dying. Because what the hell, you're already dead.

Next comes the heavenly brakes gently applied and you find yourself standing inside the pool of light. There's somebody walking toward you. At first, the somebody looks like ET waddling through all that light. You know, just a little dark, awkward silhouette. But soon ET begins to take shape. The closer it comes at you, the more it takes on a human form. Then, just like that, the silhouette becomes a real person.

It's your dad.

Holy crap, you haven't seen your dad since he bought the farm from the big C all those years ago. And the funny thing is, he's younger than you are now. He died at forty-six years old and you just turned forty-eight. Now you're older than the old man and you're standing there inside all eternity with him.

You're not sure what to do. You don't know the newly-arrived-in-heaven protocol. Do you hold out your hand for him to shake? Do you take him in your arms and embrace him? You were sort of close back on earth. But you weren't touchy feely.

You opt for the easy way out.

—Yo, what's up, Dad?

The old man is dressed in the suit you buried him in under the oak tree at the Albany Rural Cemetery. Black pin-striped double-breasted, bright red rose on the lapel, hair slicked back with Dippity-do. He looks pretty damn good for a guy who's been dead going on three decades.

—Son, I've missed you. I've been able to watch the play-by-play over the years, and I must say, life hasn't been easy for you.

OK, now you feel red-faced embarrassed. Was it possible for the old man to see everything you've done? With and without clothes on?

—You know what happened, then…to my head?

You find yourself touching the small, button-sized scar behind your right ear, where a frag of .22 caliber hollow-point penetrated your skull during an aborted suicide attempt that went bad. If any of that makes sense.

—Son, things kind of got out of control. Your wife, she had an affair with your partner. Then you fell in love with a sadly married

scarlet-haired beauty whom you could not have, and it nearly killed you both.

—You disappointed in me, Dad?

—You lived. You survived for your boy. But, Richard, you are a hopeless victim of love.

The old man is smiling at you now. You can't believe he's really there in front of you. Alive but dead. Younger but older. But time is of the essence here, and you decide to pull off at the nearest exit on this conversation and take a new route.

—What's it like being dead, Dad?

—You tell me.

—No, I mean for a long time.

—Time is a nothing here.

—Are we in heaven?

—You could say that. I believe I raised you to believe in that kind of thing.

—What should I do first?

—Nothing.

—Nothing?

—You do nothing because you're not done with life.

—Not done with life...I don't get it.

The old man's smile melts off his face. He takes a step back, purses his lips. You pick up on the old man's expression right away. It means the earth, or should you say heavenly space, is about to shift right out from under your feet.

—I'm not staying, am I, Dad?

—You're not ready, kid.

You recall the Some Young Guy your sig other was nearly tonguing inside the hospital room. You see something else too. In your dead head you see the Obama-masked mugs of those mofos who pulled you off the *street, pulled you into a back alley, kicked you in the face, kicked you in the kidneys.*

But the good news is this: if you do come back alive, you might be able to take care of some unfinished business with said Obama-masked thugs. But then something else dawns on you. It dawns on you that if your dad could see you from heaven, then maybe he can help ID the bastards who further fucked up your already fucked-up head. Masks or no masks.

—Dad, who killed me?

—You can't ask me questions like that, son. It's against the rules.

—Are they the Russians I put out of business? They had accents, I think. Or are they the on-the-take cops I exposed? Were they sent by my ex-wife to collect for back child support? Speak to me, Dad!

—You have work to do, Richard.

—What about that guy with Lola in the hospital room, Dad? Some Young Guy! You must have seen him. I couldn't get a good look at his face. At least tell me his name!

But the old man isn't talking anymore. Not about thugs; not about Lola's new lover. Maybe up in heaven that's considered cheating. He's just back-stepping, back into the light.

Correction: he's not walking so much as he's floating back into the light, his body getting smaller and smaller, his figure becoming silhouetted against the light. Until finally he becomes one with the light.

That's when something amazing happens. The light disappears. It's replaced with that tunnel, or wormhole. You're speeding through the wormhole so fast you feel the skin on your face peeling back away from your skull. That skin means you're becoming human again. And because you're human again, the lacerations on your arms begin to throb, your broken nose begins to bleed, your teeth loosen up, lips swell, your big black eye closes back up, your spleen bleeds internally, your kidneys balloon to twice their size, a big gash opens up on your right side, your temperature rises to a dangerous 103.5 degrees Fahrenheit.

Like careening out of control down a long schoolyard slide, you're going too fast. Until there's no slide left and you drop flat onto your glutes, the entirety of your 175 pounds reinjected into damaged skin and bone. You suck in a breath, open your one good eye to a blinding overhead light, and abracadabra-holy-freakin'-crap, you're alive again.

Moonlight rises.

CHAPTER 1

Life sucks. Then you die.

Or, in my case, you die and then you live.

That kinda sucks too.

The ICU is a beehive of activity.

Monitor alarms pulse.

Buzzers buzz.

Bells chime.

Nurses frantically work intravenous lines. They shout at one another. Get in one another's faces. Their words aren't exactly discernable yet. More like those weird *waa-waa* adult voices on that old *Charlie Brown Christmas* TV special. One of them even enters into this fake-as-all-hell cry, like I'm better off dead. Or maybe the drama queen just requires a little more attention than the rest of the crew. Luckily nobody's buying the pretend show of tears. They just ignore her and go about their business.

Hell is other people. I should know. I've been to heaven and back.

The tall, dark-haired doctor rushes back in, begins poking and prodding me. He shines the business end of a bright pen-light in my good eye, and I instinctively rear back against the 100 percent acrylic, allergen-free, nylon pillow.

The doc just about jumps out of his lime green Crocs.

"WE GOT A LIVE ONE!"

I can hear his voice plainly enough. It's enough to raise the dead.

"How long was he gone? Come on people. How! Long! Gone!"

Fake Cry Nurse steps up. She's young, blond, and sporting considerable cleavage beneath a white blouse, and I'm at least alive enough to feel myself getting a rise out of her. "I'm guessing just short of five minutes, Doctor." She sniffles. "His girlfriend said good-bye to him, for God's sake."

Here's what I'm thinking:

Five minutes. That's got to be a record or something, right? Book deal kind of record? Cable television movie kind of record? Somebody call an agent.

"Miracle of miracles," the doc muses, shaking his head. "Never seen anything like it."

He leans down into my ear.

"Can you hear me, Mr. Moonlight? If you can hear me, nod your head."

I take his advice, nod my head.

"Can you talk?"

I open my mouth, try to spit something out. But it all emerges as a stuttering crackle. Like my tongue has dried out and is now stuck to the back of my throat.

"Take it easy, killer. You don't need to strain yourself."

Gee, thanks, Doc.

Chin against chest, I manage a glance down at my lap. My erection is enormous. Too much blood for too little skin. The side effect of a severe concussion: spontaneous erections. The crying nurse with the cleavage can't help but notice either. She smiles, the faux crying jag all but historical fact.

"My, my...Welcome back to the land of the living...Dick."
Turning to another nurse. "Find his girlfriend! Stat!"

Yeah, that's it. Go get my girlfriend. Go get the ever-loyal
Lola. Wait till she hears I'm alive. That should be a serious
wake-up call.

Fake Cry Nurse runs out into the hall. But not before
reaching out with her right hand and giving my resurrected
Johnson a flick of her index finger. SOP for an unwanted erection under hospital circumstances. Or so my ex-wife, Lynn, the
one-time chief nurse of this very hospital used to tell me back
when we still acknowledged one another's presence on planet
earth.

I watch Johnson recede. Back to normal limp proportions.
Dead again.

As the doc exits the room, I sense some commotion coming
from down the corridor. And then there she is. Jackie O sunglasses masking her face. My girlfriend. My love. My significant
other.

Dr. Lola Ross, licensed clinical psychologist and state university professor.

She rushes to me, bends down over me, embraces me. She's
so happy I can feel her tears pouring down onto my face. Real
tears as opposed to falsies.

"You were dead, Richard! You were so very, very, very dead.
They called it, just five minutes ago. Dead. Deceased. I was
here! Right here, standing by your side."

I'm not dead anymore, I want to say. But I still can't say
squat. So I just let her cry while, out the corner of my eye, I
keep a vigil for Some Young Guy. Maybe this time I'll get a
good look at his face. But he's nowhere to be seen. Is it possible
I dreamed him all up?

The medical staff decides it's safe to leave us alone for a minute. Or maybe they're rushing out to see who will be the first to call the papers, or *Ripley's Believe It or Not*. Crap, maybe it's just time for a cig break.

We stay silent for a while. Me and sig other. Correction: me and the *former* sig other. Until, after a time, Lola separates herself from me, stands up straight. She asks me if I want a sip of water.

I manage to nod yes.

She holds a pale pink plastic cup with a straw in it directly in front of my face. I wrap my lips around the straw, sip with all my might, which ain't much. The water burns the back of my throat, but it also loosens up the concrete rigor mortis that lodged itself there when I was dead. I open my mouth, and for the first time a real voice emerges, however sandpaper rough.

"I'm baccckkkk..."

She smiles warmly, takes hold of my hand. I smell perfume. The Chanel No. 5 she splashes on herself only on special occasions. Like before we have sex for instance.

"I was about to make preparations for...your...funeral." She starts to cry again when she says the word "funeral." But all I can picture is Some Young Guy with his hand on her butt, his lips barely inches from her lips.

I try to laugh, but only manage to cough up some nasty-tasting bile. I think about confronting her about her new boyfriend. But I'm in no shape for a fight. I've just been brought back from the dead, after all. Even Lazarus must have known enough to pick his fights like his nose. There is simply a time and a place for everything, and this ain't the time for fighting. Instead, I just hold her cold clammy hand and let her sweat it out.

Lying back on the hard bed, I feel the weight of sleep consume me once more.

Moonlight head case FYI: sleep is a lot different than death. It's relaxation as opposed to total bodily freedom.

I close my good eye and drift off to the sound of Lola's voice telling me to "Sleep, Richard...Go. To. Sleep. But please don't die on me again."

As I drift off, I think, *Baby, are you gonna have some serious fucking explaining to do when I wake up, or what?*

CHAPTER 2

When I wake up again, I can see that I've been moved to another room outside of ICU. A room with a view of downtown Albany. And lucky me, I've got company. There's a big side of beef standing in the open doorway dressed in APD uniform blues and a plainclothes dick taking up space just inside the room.

I don't recognize the uniform.

Same goes for Plainclothes.

But that doesn't mean anything. I rarely have anything to do with APD's finest anymore. Not since I busted up an illegal body parts harvesting op a few years ago. Half the department was dismissed over that scandal, and the other half that remained refused to give me any work as an independent investigator. Work I relied on to pay for food and other life essentials, especially when it came to my son.

To Albany law enforcement, I'm tainted meat.

Rotten. Stinky. Untouchable.

You can be damn sure I abide by the speed limit these days, because even a simple traffic ticket promises the possibility of jail time. Especially if a cop decides to plant an ounce of pot in my trunk, or maybe slip an unlicensed hand cannon inside my glove box when I'm not looking. Truth be aired: if the cops who pulled my sad corpse out of that back alley had even the slightest idea of who it was they were rescuing, they might have kept on walking.

Listen: exposing crooked cops can cost a head-case private detective like me dearly. Cops...*SmAlbany* cops...have a way of blacklisting your ass. So when finances got so tight I had to send my six-year-old back home to his mother in Los Angeles because I couldn't afford to feed and clothe him without skipping out on the heating bill, I knew that I'd better start looking for work other than private dicking around.

But as luck would have it, I managed to score a small gig with an anonymous bar manager who claimed his abusive boss was running an illegal gambling parlor in the back of a used-car operation that he also owned right next door. Said bar manager wanted me to go undercover as the place's newest car salesman and, in the process, try to gather up enough evidence to put the boss away for good.

But I didn't even get past the job interview before I sort of managed to burn the used-car operation down while the uncle and his girlfriend were still inside it.

I know what you're thinking: that's bloody horrible.

Well, the uncle and the girlfriend tried to kill me, first by drowning me in a grease pit filled with old oil and gasoline. So they got what was coming to them.

The good news is that I solved the problem for the bar manager. Problem is, when the bar manager couldn't pay me for my services, he gave me the bar outright. Which meant that Private Detective Richard Moonlight was now the proud owner of Moonlight's Moonlit Manor.

Or Moonlight's, for short.

Place doesn't bring me a lot of money by any stretch of the imagination, but at least I can eat and pay my bills. As for my son, he's still in LA attending grammar school. Word is that I'll get him back for summer vacations. Or so his mother promised. But I'm not holding my breath since I'm still behind on my support payments. Just like the Albany cops, she considers me about one notch lower than rotting meat. You know, the kind with worms in it. But then, she never did have much of a sense of humor. Not even when she fell heels over head with my APD partner in the backseat of our assigned squad car.

Plainclothes seats himself in a chair directly across from me. He's wearing a trench coat, which he doesn't bother taking off. The insecure type, I know them well. He's about my age, with thinning gray hair slicked back against his skull. Clean shaven, blue suit underneath the trench coat, maybe picked up at a thrift shop. Sal Army, not that cheap-ass Goodwill crap. Slim black tie we all used to wear back in the eighties New Wave days. Corner barbershop groomed. He looks neat and conservative enough for a department dick.

From my bed, I shoot a glance at his wedding finger and see that it's empty. Moonlight the observant. I also see that the sun's rays haven't quite tanned the white ring-line that remains. Another newly-separated-on-the-way-to-divorce cop. Big surprise there.

"Mind if I ask you a few questions, Mr. Moonlight?"

"Dick," I offer. "Dick."

"'Scuse me?" the uniformed side of beef breaks in. He's obviously under the impression I'm trying to mess with his boss. Or maybe he's just trying to pick a fight with the near dead.

"That's my name. Dick. As in, your boss may call me Dick, as opposed to *a* dick."

Beefy Super Cop takes a step back, his face assuming a beet-red patina. Plainclothes turns around in his chair.

"Tell you what, Mike. Head down to the cafeteria and grab a coffee. I won't be long here."

Sufficiently chastised, the cop shoots me a glare, like most cops around here do now, since bringing down half their house. "You need me, Detective," he mumbles, his glare never veering from my face, "I won't be far away."

When Super Cop is gone, the detective sets his eyes back on me.

"I'm Detective Dennis Clyne," he says. Then, "I'd shake your hand, Dick, but under the circumstances…"

We both shoot a glance down at my hands, which are scraped up, the knuckles noticeably swelled. I did try to fight back against those Obamas, after all.

"No matter," I whisper, my throat still feeling like someone rubbed sandpaper against the back of it. "Go ahead and ask your questions."

Clyne reaches into his trench coat pocket, pulls out a small spiral notepad like the reporters used before they could record everything you said with iPhones. He flips open the top, gives the blank page a quick look-see.

"Give it to me from the start."

That's when I ask him for a drink of water.

"What?" He makes a frown, shakes his head like my request doesn't compute.

I tell him to pour me some water from the pitcher set out on the little table beside me. Pour it into the plastic cup. Then

I ask him to put a straw into it and place it toward my mouth so I can drink it. Can't spill my guts to him with a dry mouth.

His eyes go all aflutter.

"Maybe we should call a nurse."

"*Youuu cannn dooooo eeeet,*" I encourage in a raspy voice.

Exhaling like my ex-wife used to do when I asked for morning sex, he gets up, pours the water into the cup, tosses the straw into it, and sets it under my chin.

"Pillow."

More exhaling.

"Need a little more elevation."

I sit up as far as I can. With his free hand he shoves one of the acrylic pillows down behind the other, compacts it tight. He exhales for a third time and holds the water in front of my face again. I tongue the straw, wrap my lips around it, and suck. The water burns when it goes down my pipes, but it offers some relief too.

"We good to go here, Moonlight?" Clyne poses, wide-eyed and tight-lipped, the agitation in his voice as plain as the white walls. "I seriously don't have all afternoon."

"You give new meaning to the term public servant," I say, sitting back, the straw sticking to my lips until it comes loose and drops to the floor. "What's on your mind?"

The detective sits back down, crosses his legs. When his pant legs rise up, I can see he's wearing white tennis socks. I'll bet his wife never would have let him out of the house like that. But then, what do I know? He sees that I see that he has white socks on, and he quickly uncrosses his legs, sets his feet flat on the floor.

He picks up his notebook, like it helps jumpstart his memory.

"You were attacked. Physically assaulted by roughens in downtown Albany. Broadway at the corner of Beaver. How many were there?"

"The *roughens* you mean?"

He nods.

"Three."

He lifts his writing hand, makes a curling motion with the wrist. Like he wants me to elaborate.

"They were big, I think. Dressed all in black. Jeans, boots, sweatshirts. President Obama masks covered their faces. These goofy rubber masks that made them look like cartoon presidents."

"How old?"

"Young enough to do this to me."

He looks me up and down, starts to write something. "Between twenty and seventy," he says under his breath. "All male. That pretty much narrows it, Moonlight."

"Look, they were using those handheld electronic machines for talking. You know, the little machines that throat cancer survivors use after their voice box has been removed."

"You mean a voice synthesizer."

"Yeah, one of those."

"So, they beat you with them?"

I can't help but crack a smile. I might even laugh if I don't know how much it'll hurt. The brokenhearted Clyne has a sense of humor, after all. Laughter: the best medicine. Jack Daniels might argue with that.

"No, Clyne. They pressed them up under their jaws when they spoke. Came out all electronic. They were masking their voices."

"American voices?"

"They were definitely speaking English. I think. Or..."

"Which is it, Mr. Moonlight?"

"Some of the words came out sounding stranger than others. And only one of them actually said anything. Maybe the voice was foreign. Foreign for Albany, anyway. But the voice machines made it hard to make out. Plus they were pounding the snot out of me. But for sure the voice wasn't young or old."

"Interesting."

"Glad I'm keeping it colorful for you. I was a cop like you once too. It's not hard to tell how old someone is by the sound of their voice."

"But it's hard for you, Moonlight."

"OK, I'll own that one."

"I get it. Twenty to seventy. Like I already said."

"Yeah, somewhere in there. More like forty I'd say. All around."

"OK, we'll go with that. Four-Oh. Next question. You piss anybody off lately?"

"How's about who haven't I pissed off lately?"

He rolls his eyes. "Of course," he says. "The Russians, the body parts, the APD cop thing, the local mob who used to own your new bar. You've been fighting a multifront war, Moonlight. I seem to recall coming across a headline or two in the *Times Union* archives. 'Moonlight Falls' or something like that."

"How is it you weren't a part of all that, Clyne?"

"Just transferred to Albany six months ago. Came up from Yonkers. But I'm the type who likes to do his research."

"You came up *here*? Nobody fucking comes up *here*."

"My wife wanted to raise a family up *here* in Albany. The country, so to speak."

I eye his ring finger again. The white line.

"Your wife," I say. It's a question.

His face goes cadaver stiff. "Oh you *are* a detective." Glares at me, then sighs. "My marital status ain't none of your god-damned business, Moonlight."

"Been there, done that. Just trying to help." I raise my right hand, touch the bullet scar beside my right earlobe. An involuntary act, especially when it comes to talking about infidelity. Mine or my ex's.

"You shot yourself in the head a few years ago and survived," Clyne says, his eyes focused on the visible scar in a solemn way that makes me think he's no stranger to contemplating suicide himself. "Neat trick," he adds.

"It was an accident. And it was only a small piece of .22 cal hollow-point that pierced my skull...That's my story, anyway."

"You most definitely lived."

"Opted out at the last second. In my head, I saw my little boy staring down at his dead dad. Pulled the barrel away, but I was drunk, and my trigger finger didn't get the memo. Ninety-five percent of the bullet shattered against my skull. But a small sliver entered into my brain, lodged itself beside my cerebral cortex. Can't be operated on. Sometimes I get short-term memory loss. Other times, I run the risk of a stroke. I could die, I guess, pretty much at any time, with or without getting the crap beat out of me by a bunch of Obamas holding voice machines up against their throats."

"Yet you go on living."

"Like the Energizer bunny."

He stands up, shoves the notebook back into an inside pocket of his trench coat.

"That's it?" I pose.

"For now. Sounds like those three perps could have been anyone, black or white or yellow, knowing how many enemies you have in Albany." Cocking his head. "Could even be a random act of violence. Lotsa people out of work these days. Prices going up. Gas through the roof. Especially if these guys turn out to be foreigners."

"How ironical," I point out. "However, they never took my wallet. But one of them did say something I understood perfectly well."

Pulling his notepad back out. "Shoot."

"They told me to stay away from Peter Czech."

He seems taken aback for a beat or two. Like I suddenly passed gas.

"Spell it," he says.

I do it.

"So who's Peter Czech?"

"Wheelchair-bound young guy came to me a few days ago. Asked me to find his father. Claims he was given up for adoption immediately upon birth. Twenty-five years ago or thereabouts. He did some snooping on the Web, found out it's possible his old man still lives in Albany, right under his mustached upper lip."

"What about his adoptive parents? They still alive?"

"Not according to him. Died in a car accident in the nineties. Head-on collision. Hit-and-run. Never found the guy who was driving the truck. Biological mother's dead too."

"You might have told me all this when we started."

Me, pursing my lips. "I tend to forget things sometimes. My head...it can't always be trusted. Besides, I haven't really done any work on the project yet, since I'm not entirely sure I want it. Which I might have explained to the Obama boys if they'd only have given me the chance to talk."

He raises his right hand, pokes his skull behind his earlobe, in the exact place where the little piece of bullet entered my head.

"The memory...she comes and goes," I say.

"Like my wife," he says.

Beefy Officer Mike shows back up at the door.

"Everything OK, Detective?"

"Yeah," Clyne answers. "Just a minute." Then back to me. "Care to give me the phone number and address of this, ah, Peter Czech?"

"Nope."

"Even if it might lead to the assholes who did this to you?"

"Yup."

"Client confidentiality, right?"

"Yup."

"At least think about it?"

"Yup."

Reaching into his pants pocket, he tosses a business card onto my lap. "I'll be in touch," he warns. "In the meantime, watch your back. The enemies you've made in Albany are a lot more dangerous than that piece of lead in your brain. And that's saying something."

He turns, walks out the door. Officer Mike lags behind, standing in the open door, filling it like a giant pig in a big blue blanket. He smiles at me, exposing every single one of his grinding teeth. He bobs his head and glares at me. If we were back on the schoolyard, he'd be the big fat bully who stares you down from across the jungle gym before beating the lunch money out of you. I hate bullies.

"Excuse me, Officer Mike," I speak up, feeling a telltale dizziness swimming around my battered brain. "Would you mind finding me a new straw for my water?"

He raises up his right hand, flashes me his middle digit.

"There's your fucking straw." He smiles. "Suck on that for a while...Dick."

He walks.

I guess he told me off but good, even if dick jokes are totally nineties.

The dizziness in my head gets worse. My vision begins to come and go. Like a Maglite with the batteries about to go on me.

I call for a nurse. The one with the glorious cleavage. But I pass out before the heavenly vision can come to my rescue.

CHAPTER 3

You're on a lifeboat that's bobbing in the middle of the Atlantic Ocean. Just a plain old wooden lifeboat like the kind they somehow forgot to bring along on the Titanic. *On one side of you sits Lola. On the other, her new boyfriend. The faceless Some Young Guy. Only this guy isn't faceless. He's got Detective Clyne's sad face.*

You're naked, the sun beating down on your skin and flesh like a broiler oven on French fries. You're also thirsty as all hell. Desert sand parched.

Lola's like ten years younger than she is now. A fucking pulse-throbbing, heart-aching vision, even if she is but a figment of your imagination. She's wearing this smoking-hot red thong-kini, like she picked it special for the dream, and she's sipping a bottle of cold beer.

Dos Equis.

Some Young Clyne is naked too, and he's sporting this huge-ass boner. Just the biggest banana-shaped man sausage you've ever seen. It makes you want to cry, the thing is so fucking big, while your own looks like a shriveled raisin in the sun.

Maybe the hot sun is beating down on you, but your right side is on fire. It feels like a hot poker is being jammed through your skin into your kidney. You look to your right and you can see that Some Young Clyne is sticking you with a bowie knife. He's got it thrust into your side, the jagged spine of the blade scraping against your bottommost rib.

Lola is laughing, sipping her beer. She takes her top off, allows her bouncy white titties to hang out. "Need to get catch some UVs," she says, running the pad of her index finger over sexy red lips, then over her mams, making those nipples scrumptiously pert and perky. Like she's nineteen all over again.

"Don't distract me," says Some Young Clyne, his big boner bobbing up and down while he works. "I gotta get this thing out without popping it."

You're in agony, red lights flashing in your eyes. He's ramming the blade in deeper and deeper, until he reaches in with his hand, pulls something out...Something goopy, raw, and meaty.

It's your kidney.

Your. Fucking. Kidney.

He holds it up like a triumphant Apache warrior holding up the still-beating heart of General Custer.

"Nice work, baby," Lola cheerfully utters while grabbing hold of his cock. "Now how's about an ice-cold beer and a little stress release to go with it."

I wake up to the scent of leather.

A hand is covering my mouth. A black-gloved hand, pressed down tight. One of those men-in-black Obama goons is standing on my right side, another on the left, and one at the foot of the bed. I peer down at my side. The Obama on my right flank is sticking me with a scalpel, jabbing the blade inside a fresh, three-stacked-rib-length gash that's been sutured with a staple gun. He's flicking the topmost staple and issuing a heartfelt giggle each time he does it.

Sick goon at the foot of the bed holds that cancer voice machine up to his throat.

"You should have stayed dead, dude," he says, voice sounding like a computer. Sort of like that famous wheelchair physics guy, Stephen Hawking. Stephen Hawking with a foreign accent. Now I'm convinced the Obamas aren't exactly American nationals, after all, just like Clyne was getting at earlier.

I want to reach out, grab hold of the emergency nurse call. But I can't move. I can't talk. The stabs of the scalpel take my breath away. The flicking of the topmost staple makes me see through a sheen of red. I'm choking. Choking on my own pain.

"Peter Czech...he was here, dude?" Obama says. "He give you something, yes? What is it he give you, Mister Moonlight, dude?"

Scalpel Man pulls back on the blade. The relief is instantaneous. I'm able to swallow, able to moisten the back of my throat.

"I don't know," I tell him, surprised at the sound of my own voice, now that it's an entire octave higher than normal. "No one's been here."

Flick goes the staple. I see red. Body burning electric.

"Liar. We watch him come here, dude. Two hours ago. We fucking watch him. We think it is possible sneaky bastard give you a...a...a...what you call it...a *flesh box*. What does *flesh box* contain, dude?"

"No, stupid," interrupts the Obama on my left. "*Zeepy box*. That's what it is. It's possible Czech give him a *zeepy box*, stupid motherfucker."

"Fuck cares what it's called in America!" barks the scalpel man.

I'm trying to make out where these men come from. But it's tough to understand their voices through the synths. It screws up the sound of their words more than they're capable of doing on their own. And anyhow, I don't see a box of any size, shape, or form inside the room. I don't see a flesh box or a zeepy box or a shoebox or anything resembling a box.

I look one way, then the other.

I try to get up, but I can't budge myself from the bed. I just don't see a box or I'd gladly give it to them so long as it'll make them stop digging at me with that scalpel.

This room isn't big. There's no storage. Wouldn't a box be set out in plain sight? Is it possible Czech was here and I can't remember? There's a bullet frag stuck in my brain, and I just had my head bashed in by these same Obama look-alikes. Yes, it's entirely possible I suffered another memory lapse.

"If you see what you're looking for inside this room," I say and swallow, "you are most certainly welcome to have it. It'll be my gift to you."

"What do you do with it, dude? Where do you hide box, dude?"

"I. Don't. Have. A. Box."

The scalpel is inserted, the blade flicks the staple, and this time doesn't the mofo pop out.

I hear the tinny jingle of a single medical staple hitting the hard floor.

Then I see several rapid-fire flashes of red just before passing out.

When I come to, the Obamas are standing at the foot of the bed. One of them is looking out through a crack in the door. They obviously know that someone is coming, and that means they have to exit the premises. Pronto.

"We'll be back, Mister Moonlight," warns the lead Obama. "And we want what we come for, yes, dude?"

"By all means...dude." But I have no idea what box, and even more, no idea about my new client Peter Czech having paid me a visit.

The Obamas scoot out the door.

I roll onto my good side and heave all over the bed.

CHAPTER 4

A few minutes later Lola walks in, carrying a white vase filled with fresh flowers. She takes one look at me and drops the flowers to the floor. The vase shatters.

So do my nerves.

I don't realize it, but the little staple flicking/popping incident has left a puddle of blood on the bed. On the opposite side sits a pool of my own brown bile.

Moonlight the attractive.

I sit up, feeling more of that electric pain shoot up and down my side. I pull off the covers and somehow swing my legs around.

"You're out of your head!" Lola says, voice trembling.

I suck down a breath and work up the strength needed to pull out the intravenous lines.

"No, I'm out of my *bed*, and we have to go. I stay here, I'm a dead man."

"Richard, it's the hospital. You *leave*, you're a dead man."

I slide off the bed. Stand. A bit wobbly. But once I get my breath back, I know I can manage without falling flat on my face. I shuffle to the closet, find my clothes. I toss them to Lola.

"Help me with these. I'm telling, not asking."

She's still wearing those Jackie Os. Tight jeans, black sweater. Hair long and pulled back in a ponytail. I can't help but wonder where Some Young Guy has run off to. Or if he even exists in the real world. Maybe I dreamed him up in the first place. The brain plays tricks on you when it's deprived of oxygen.

"Can you please tell me what's going on?"

I tear off the gown and reveal yet another uncontrollable erection. Doesn't matter at this point. Lola has seen it a thousand times before. It ain't all that much to look at, even at full mast. Maybe that's the problem. Maybe that's why Lola has turned to Some Young Guy. Maybe Johnson and I are just not good enough for her.

"Help me into my pants."

She hesitates.

"Like now!"

She bends down with my Levi's in hand. There's blood on them. She holds the pants like you would for a child who's too young to dress himself. I step into the pant leg. More electric pain. I step into the other leg and, with Lola's help, pull them up and over my manhood.

That's when the nurse steps in, her eyes shifting from the shattered ruins of a broken vase on the floor to me. She's the good-looking, short blond nurse. The one with the cleavage.

"Oh no you're not!"

She lunges at me, grabs hold of my arm. I pull away.

"A man was here earlier. In a wheelchair. Did you see him?"

She goes wide-eyed. I'm trying not to look down into her cleavage. But it's like trying not to look at parallel Mount Everests while standing in front of them.

"Yes. He said he was a friend. You spoke with him for a while." Eyes back on the wilted flowers and shattered ceramic. Then back on me. "Did he give you anything? Anything I should know about?"

A silent beat. "Why are you asking me that?"

Shaking her head, she says, "You have a brain injury. You obviously don't remember anything." Her eyes shift down to my midsection. "You're getting spontaneous erections due to a bruised thalamus. Not an ideal situation for someone who can suffer a stroke at any time. Get back in bed."

I glance downward. Just as I thought. I'm showing.

She goes to grab me again, but this time I take her hand and hold it. I shoot a glance at Lola. "Lo, watch the door."

She does it.

"It's possible the man in the wheelchair gave me some kind of box, or something that looks like a box or a package. I don't see it here. Did you take it? Is that why you're asking me if he gave me something?"

"You're hurting me," she says, trying to free her hand. "I don't remember a box. Do you? Could it be around here?"

I shake my head. My side feels squishy and liquidy. I know I'm bleeding, the blood running from my side down my right leg.

"Some men came to see me just a few minutes ago. They were dressed in black and wearing masks like President Obama. Did you see them too?"

"Mr. Moonlight, I've been standing out at that desk all morning, and I did not see any men wearing masks. My brain is perfectly normal and I would recall that."

They must have gotten in through the service elevator somehow. Or the stairs. One at a time. Maybe even wore lab coats to make themselves look like hospital support staff.

I let her go, grabbing the rest of my clothing.

"I'm leaving and don't try and stop me, understand? There's no law against me leaving. I need you to grab me a wheelchair. Now. Please. Please. Now."

Nurse shakes her head, bites down on her lip. She slips past Lola, and just for a moment the two women pause to glare at each other, almost like they're about to engage in conversation.

But without saying a word, Nurse heads out into the hall, returning right away with a wheelchair, the letters AMC stenciled on the back.

"You're making a huge mistake," Lola says as I ease down into the chair. "You should listen to the nurse instead of just staring goo-goo eyed at her boobs. You have a preexisting brain injury. You could stroke at any time. You could die. Again."

I ask Lola to place a blanket over me. She grabs the one off the bed, steps around the puddle of broken glass and flowers, and drapes it over my lap.

"Dead again," I say to Nurse. "Been there, done that." Then to Lola. "Let's go."

"One of these times, Mr. Moonlight," Nurse says, "you're not going to wake up from being dead."

"He who dies today is quit for next," I say, wheeling myself through the open door. "Shakespeare said that. Or maybe it was Ernest Hemingway. In any event, they're both dead now."

"So are you," Nurse says, "one way or another."

I don't like the way she says it. Death isn't something to joke around with. But then life...life is a different story. Especially my own train wreck of an existence. Now *there's* something to laugh about.

CHAPTER 5

We make it to the elevator without anyone, doctor or nurse, giving us a second thought. Down on the hospital's ground floor level, Lola pushes my chair slowly, casually, as though she's taking me for a stroll in the hospital courtyard for some much deserved fresh air.

If I close my eyes right now, I swear I'll fall asleep and not wake up for three days. Or maybe at all. Moonlight the near dead.

It's almost a letdown how easily we make it to Lola's ride. Without even a single white-smocked doctor giving us any kind of hassle whatsoever. The half dozen we pass by on our way down the narrow corridor toward the electronic sliding doors simply issue kind bedside smiles and keep on their merry way.

Stat!

By the time Lola helps me up into the passenger seat of her Hummer, the blood oozing out my side has soaked through the towel. My erection has subsided, thank God, but I'm also beginning to feel lightheaded, which isn't anything unusual for me, new concussion or no new concussion. But I know that if I don't get that gash in my side stitched back up soon, I'll pass out not from simple exhaustion but from blood loss.

"Head straight to Georgie's," I say through gritted teeth.

Lola gives me no argument. But I can tell from the tight-as-a-tick expression on her face that she isn't liking any of this. She even opens her mouth once as if to say something, reveal some kind of truth, or at the very least, give me a good tongue-lashing. Maybe she knows that I know that's she's been cheating and maybe now she wants to confess. But she doesn't confess. She just clams up on me again. In the end she just sighs, turns the big eight-cylinder over, and backs out of the parking spot.

When she pulls out onto the road, I can't help but spot them sitting inside an unmarked Chevy: Detective Clyne and his driver, Officer Mike. At first I can't be sure they've caught sight of me. But when big Mike holds his hand out the open window and flips me off for the second time in twenty-four hours, I'm pretty damned sure I've been spotted by the APD, the same crime stoppers who rescued me from the Albany back alley in the first place. Against their better judgment, no doubt.

No matter what happens from this point on, I'll bet the nonexistent mortgage on Moonlight's Moonlit Manor that those two cops won't be far from my tail. What I can't decide, how-ever, is if a cop tail is a good thing or a bad thing for a marked man like me.

CHAPTER 6

First things first: I ask Lola if I can borrow her cell phone since mine is nowhere to be found. Reluctantly, she hands it to me. Like I'm gonna get blood on it or something.

My new client Peter Czech's number is printed on his business card, which has been stuffed in my jeans pocket since he gave it to me a few days ago. I pull out the crumpled card, read the number, stuff it back inside the pocket, and try to swallow the throbbing pain in my side.

I dial the number, wait for a pickup.

When it comes I don't give him a chance to say hello.

"Czech, did you come see me in the hospital?"

"How are you, Mr. Moonlight?" he responds in his happy, smiley, singsong voice. I can just picture him smoothing out his mustache, seated in his wheelchair, the wheels of which might be locked in front of a massive, black nuclear submarine. All around him stand HEPA-suited engineers working on the sub's nuclear core while military personnel busy themselves by arming the missiles and warheads. I'm not sure if the picture I'm creating in my mind is entirely accurate. But it feels kind of accurate, in a Hollywood sort of way.

"You visit me?" I press.

"I did come to see you just this morning. Remember? I was concerned about you. You were groggy, but awake. We laughed about your nurse with the...uhhh...nice breasts."

"Breasts," I say, picturing the small blond nurse. "How'd you find out I was hurt?"

"This is *SmAlbany*, after all. Word gets around quick. Cops reported the news to the *Times Union* after they found you half dead. I read the police blotters off the Internet edition. Old habit of mine. It's fun. I'm surprised you don't read them."

"Albany's small, all right. But not small enough for you to ever run into your father?"

"Gee, Mr. Moonlight. It's like I said. I'm not sure I would know my father if I were sitting next to him at the Miss Albany Diner. That's why I've hired you."

Lola's driving, listening, white-knuckle gripping the steering wheel like she's trying to fly a plane that wants to crash.

"OK," I say, "I get it. You came to see me. We conversed about a nurse's tits. What the hell else did we talk about?"

Lola exhales angrily. I cup my hand over the mouthpiece. "Sorry, Lo," I whisper in her direction.

"You were pretty out of it. It wasn't much of a conversation, to be honest. I only stayed a couple of minutes."

"Did you give me something? A box?"

He hesitates for a weighted beat.

"You still there, Czech?"

"Still here, yes sirree. No, I don't recall giving you anything. Not even a stick of gum. Not that you could chew it without choking anyway. You were on your back, dead to the world." He follows up with a chuckle. Guy's responsible for me nearly buying the farm and he's getting a big kick out of it. If he were in front of me now I'd tip over his wheelchair. OK, maybe not.

"You're sure."

"I'm a nuclear engineer. I'm paid well, both for my precision and razor-sharp recall."

"Good enough. Oh, and Czech, do you actually work on the submarines themselves? Do they have any at the plant?"

He laughs again. Guy's just full of good humor today.

"We work mostly on computer-simulated models. CAD programs. If you recall, the Knolls atomic plant resides on the Mohawk River, so it's possible we have a nuclear sub or two in our possession. But..." He lets the thread trail off.

"But I'm not supposed to know about that, am I?"

"Correctamundo!" he barks.

Mr. Precision, revealing national security tidbits like that over his cell.

"I'll be in touch, Czech."

"I hope you find Daddy."

Daddy...

I hang up.

In the split second before I hand the phone back to Lola, the screen that represents my call to Czech disappears. That's when I catch a quick glimpse of her phone call log. The number she connected with last, just prior to the phone call I made to Czech. According to the readout, the number was pulled from her stored speed-dial list.

It says, "My Father."

CHAPTER 7

We ride in silence until we hit New Scotland Avenue. Me thinking about how Lola never mentioned her father, beyond once telling me that he died a long time ago. I might mention seeing the speed dial with the title "My Father" on it in big-ass letters, but like my interest in Some Young Guy, I choose to hold off. Maybe "My Father" is just a spiritual friend of hers, like a priest or a rabbi. But then I've been led to believe that Lola doesn't believe in God. And the way the listing is so coldly rendered.

My Father... As if she were saying, *My Cancer...*

Anyway, Lola has a life separate from mine—separate from *ours*, I should say. OK, whatever. That doesn't change the fact that clearly something is up with my girlfriend, and I'm not about to confront her with it until I'm good and prepared, not half dead and bleeding out.

But then quite suddenly, Lola's own curiosity kills the cat. Or in this case, the inquiring clinical psychologist, and she finally speaks up.

"What's happening here, Richard? You were pronounced dead. Beaten to death by three men wearing masks. Those same men came for you again. They could have killed you on the spot. But they didn't."

"That's because they want something from me now. I'm dead. I can't give it to them." I press the blood-soaked towel tighter against my side. "They want whatever is inside a box. Only I don't remember a box, and I don't remember a man named Peter Czech coming to my hospital room to see me. That's why I needed to call him."

"Did this man actually come to see you?"

"So he says."

"Did he give you anything?"

"He claims he didn't, and that he's a man of precision, so he would certainly recall giving me a gift. Apparently we had a conversation about my nurse."

She exhales again. Time to stop mentioning the nurse with the ample chest.

"Your head," Lola says, pulling a right onto a West Albany street congested with bungalows and townhouses on both sides. "It's not right. You've suffered yet another concussion. That's on top of the bullet in your brain. What you're doing now, leaving the hospital like that...it's suicidal."

Her message isn't lost on me. Me, the suicide survivor. Me, the dead man come back to life. The head case convinced I spotted my girlfriend kissing Some Young Guy. Or about to kiss him, anyway.

"If you're worried about me living out a death wish, you can breathe easy. I'm trying to survive, not die again."

She nods.

"So who's Peter Czech?"

"A client. New client. Came to me late last week. Said he pulled my name from out of the phone book."

"You believe that?" She shoots me a pair of squinty, disbelieving eyes.

"Can happen. Lots of people still use the phone book instead of Google."

"You wouldn't show up on Google. That's how little private investigation work you get these days."

I proceed to tell her what I know about Czech.

He's a man who's paralyzed from the waist down. A man of about thirty who crashed his car four years ago while driving back to Albany after a drunk night on the town in Saratoga Springs. Fell asleep at the wheel, drove across the median into the oncoming traffic. The pickup truck he collided with nearly split him in half when it hit his Buick four-door. The driver of the pickup bought the farm. But the only thing that kept Czech alive was his drunken state and the fact that his speed had been reduced to a crawl. The booze kept him loose during the point of impact. Otherwise, he might have been a dead man.

He phoned me five days ago, asked me if he could meet me at my bar after work that evening. I told him I wasn't doing much PI work lately, but he asked me to hear him out. I didn't argue.

When he arrived, I was surprised to see him in a wheelchair. He'd sounded so assertive and confident over the phone. So tall and broad, you might say. But I didn't know anything about his history, about the accident. We took the table in the back after I told him that it's reserved for me and for me alone, even though the place was pretty much empty. Empty, that is, except for Uncle Leo, the gray-haired Korean War vet who maintains a stool of honor at the far corner of the old wood bar.

We gathered round my table, and he introduced himself as Peter Czech and held his hand out for me to shake. The hand was thin and crooked, like a twisted tree limb. I could tell there must have been a time when it didn't work very well, and that it must have taken a hell of a lot of therapy to get it to work even a little bit right. As for his left hand, he kept that tucked up tight to his midsection, palm inverted awkwardly upward.

He was chewing an enormous wad of Juicy Fruit, and he told me he was an employee of the Knolls Atomic Research Facility in Schenectady. A chief engineer who helped design propulsion systems for Uncle Sam's nuclear submarine arsenal. His appearance fit the bill: brown slacks, white shirt, brown tie, plastic pencil holder stuffed into the left-hand pocket, black hair to match his eyes and slicked back with gel, trimmed mustache over a thin upper lip. He had a BlackBerry mobile phone stuffed inside his jacket pocket, which he kept retrieving and replacing, like he was obsessed with it or the person who might be trying to contact him.

For shits and giggles, I told him I didn't think the US still maintained an active nuclear sub force now that the threat from the Russian Bear had given way to radical Islamist terrorists. But he shook his head with vehemence.

"The nuclear submarine program is alive and deadly," he assured me with some heat in his quick-speaking Juicy Fruit voice. "And so are the dozens of nuclear warheads it carries. Tridents, ICBMs, Minute Men...you name it. We get another 9/11, Mr. Moonlight, you can betcha one of my subs will delight in lighting up Iran. Or maybe Northern Pakistan. Take your pick."

"Call me Moonlight," I told him, lighting what's become a rare smoke for me these days. "So what brings you around my bar?"

Raising one of those crooked hands.

"Mind if I have a drink?"

I felt myself smiling. Ironically. Booze almost killed him once. Indirectly, I guess. In technical terms, the truck had nearly killed him. But his condition...the fact that he would never use his legs again was all about the booze.

"Where're my manners," I said, standing up. "What's your pleasure, Mr. Czech?"

"Jack and Coke," he said, that boyish smile on his face revealing fine, straight white teeth. Czech must have had good parents. Parents with enough cash to send him to orthodontists.

I started toward the bar to mix his drink.

"Oh and hey, Mr. Moonlight," he said over his shoulder while pulling out his BlackBerry again. "Can you make it a big one?" He raised both crooked hands and made like he was measuring the size of something.

"Sure thing," I told him, and made him a drink inside a beer pint that had a worn Pabst Blue Ribbon logo pasted to it.

I remembered the hands again, so I stuck a straw in it without asking him if he wanted a straw in it, and brought it to him. When I sat back down I took a hit off my still-lit smoke, set it back down in the metal ashtray, and decided not to smoke any more of it.

"Your story," I said, exhaling a cloud of blue smoke. "Let's hear it."

"I'd like you to find my father," he said matter-of-factly. I noticed that in the time I'd made his drink he'd ditched the Juicy Fruit, which suited me just fine. He took hold of his Jack and Coke with two trembling hands, greedily mouthed the straw, and sucked a major hit off it. By the time he came back up for air, the drink was a third gone.

"You lost your dad?" I said.

"I never knew him," he explained, retrieving, observing, and quickly shoving the BlackBerry back inside his jacket yet again. "I was removed from his custody at birth. You see, my mother gave me up for adoption. Both she and my dad were too young to take care of me. So the story goes."

"What's his name?"

"Harvey Rose. It's possible he is, or *was*, an accountant in Albany. But there are many accountants in Albany and a couple of men named Harvey Rose who are most definitely not the one." He spelled out the last name for me, which wasn't necessary. I wrote it down on a bar napkin, stuffed it into my pocket.

"What about your mom?"

"She's dead."

"You know that for sure?"

"My mother confirmed it for me many years ago." Smiling again. "My adoptive mom, that is. She told me my biological mother had died of cancer back when I was fifteen. She thought I should know, so that I didn't harbor false hope of ever being reunited with her."

"Wow, your adoptive mom must have been all heart."

He laughed, took another hit off the drink, this time leaving it half empty. Or full, depending upon how you looked at it.

"She was a good mom," he said, smiling. "Just different. She was from Russia and so was my adoptive father. Muscovites. They'd escaped the Berlin Wall somehow in the late seventies and made it over to the land of the free and the home of the brave. They made a life for themselves here by going to school and educating themselves. By the time they adopted me over twenty-five years ago, my dad was employed at Knolls Atomic as a nuclear engineer. So, you could say, Mr. Moonlight, that I'm continuing the family tradition. My adoptive parents were hard workers and straightforward people. When there was something they wanted you to know, they just told you. No sugarcoating it. That's the Russian way."

"Back to your biological father," I said. "Why do you want to find him now?"

For the first time, his smile faded. He sucked down the rest of his drink.

"It's personal, Mr. Moonlight," he said, setting the empty glass back down with both, now steady, hands.

"Pardon me," I said, stamping out the still-lit cig. "But there's something we have to get straight. If you want to hire me, I need to know that you can trust me and I can trust you."

"I understand," he said with a grin.

"Good. No lies or fibs or hiding important tidbits from me for whatever reason."

He stared intently at what was left of his drink. Not too much. I got the message. I got up, mixed him another one, weaker this time. I put a fresh straw in it and set it down in front of him. Then I sat back down.

"As you might no doubt guess, my father will be getting on in years. I estimate him to be about seventy-six now, or thereabouts—"

Raising my hands, I told him to hold it while I got up, grabbed some paper napkins from behind the bar, popped a new beer for Uncle Leo, and planted myself back in front of Czech.

"Seventy-six," I repeated under my breath.

"I know he will die sooner or later and I simply want to meet with him, make some kind of peace with him...his existence."

"You've never spoken with him?"

He shook his head, sipped his new drink, slower this time.

"Never. According to my adoptive parents, I only know that he lived in this area and worked as an accountant, first with the federal government. Department of Military Affairs, I believe. The same department that oversees my operation at Knolls. Then he went to work for himself."

"Both you and your father worked at Knolls, yet you've never run into him?"

"Not that I know of. I'm not sure we'd know one another, Mr. Moonlight. But I do know that my father knew him, and perhaps that's how the whole adoption issue began in the first place."

"And his name is really Harvey Rose?" I asked.

He smiled. "Really, Mr. Moonlight, I just told you his name. You wrote it down on a napkin. I'm not making it up. That would be counterproductive. I'm an engineer, after all."

He had a point. I did just write it down, and he was an engineer. Silly me. "Why not just conduct your own search on the Internet?"

"I've already exhausted my computer search. The Harvey Roses I come up with are most definitely not him."

"How do you know?"

He smiled, upper lip hidden under that thin mustache. "I just know." Shaking his head. "My father is not listed on the Internet."

Czech's gut must have been speaking to him. I still wasn't all that thrilled about the Internet myself, even if it had taken over everyone's lives. "How can you be sure your dad still lives in the Albany area at all? How do you know he's even alive?"

"I can't be," he said. "In fact, I should tell you that there is yet one more Harvey Rose, who is listed as deceased by the Albany County Hall of Records. Died years ago. But I know in my gut that my father is alive." Another Jack and Coke smile. "Must have something to do with the blood-is-thicker-than-water thing."

"Must be," I said. "Had the dead Rose been an accountant?"

"Information I got online didn't say one way or another. He was just listed as a 'local businessman.' " He made pretend quotation marks with the fingers on his right hand when he said "local businessman."

"Any clue as to what he might look like? That is, assuming he's alive and just a very private, unlisted, off-the-Google-radar human being."

Czech reached into his pocket, pulled out a small photograph, and handed it to me.

I stared down at an old, black-and-white image of a hospital room. There was no one lying in the bed, but the sheets and blankets were tossed about, as though whoever had been lying in there had either left the room or been dismissed somehow.

A young woman and a man occupied the center of the shot. They were holding a newborn baby who was bundled up in white blankets. You couldn't see his or her face, but I'm assuming the baby was Peter Czech.

Standing to the left of the would-be father was a tall man, who was older than the couple. He had black hair, a receding hairline, and thick eyebrows—thicker than thick, and raised up on both ends, like they'd been pasted on that way. He was wearing a business suit, and he was devoid of a smile. In fact, the young couple wasn't smiling either. They were looking at the camera rather apprehensively.

That's when it dawned on me that the mother who'd borne this child—the wife or girlfriend of devil eyebrows—wasn't in the picture. I looked again at that just-recently-vacated-looking bed. She hadn't gone far, probably. Bathroom run? Or—could she be behind the camera?

That seemed a stretch. I couldn't imagine a mother giving away her child in the first place, but to record the transaction for posterity was mind-boggling. Plus, she'd be in a hell of a lot of pain to play photographer. Must be the photographer was a nurse.

Had the unseen mother and devil-eyebrowed father entered into some kind of contract or legal arrangement to have a baby for this Russian couple? I wanted to ask Czech about the possibility, but decided not to. I didn't want to hurt him, and what difference did it make how the baby came about anyway? It wouldn't affect his need to search for his maker. Not if he wanted to find his father badly enough, which he apparently did.

I went to give him back his photograph.

"You keep it," he insisted. "You're going to need it if you're going to find him."

I stuffed the picture in the left chest pocket of my black leather jacket.

"You live close by?"

"Orchard Grove Road. North Albany. Been there for almost two years now." Back to smiling cheerfully. "Hey, it's my first house. I'm pretty proud of it."

Once more he checked his BlackBerry, and judging by his now disappointed expression, once more he saw that nobody was looking for him. So once more he replaced it inside his jacket pocket.

"Buck-fifty per day," I said, getting to the business part of the conversation. "Plus expenses. I find your dad, dead or alive, I receive a ten percent bonus or a minimum of a thousand dollars. I take a thousand up front as a retainer."

Czech thought it over, nodded his head once or twice. "Agreed. Under one condition."

"That is?"

"You let me buy you a drink right now."

I smiled. I didn't like overly friendly clients. Rather, I didn't trust them. But what the hell. I was dry and it was the end of the day.

"Agreed," I said, taking his scrawny hand in mine. I released it as fast as I could without being impolite. It felt like a dead, overgrown chicken's foot.

He wheeled himself around and made his way to the bar. I went around to the cooler, uncapped another beer for Uncle Leo and one for me. Then I made a third drink for Czech with another new straw and handed it down to him.

"So what shall we drink to?" Czech asked, while retrieving his checkbook from one of his jacket pockets.

"How's about the Korean War!" Uncle Leo shouted. "We really gave it to those commie bastards up on Pork Chop Hill all summer, the year of our Lord 19 and 53! The great Gregory Peck made a terrific motion picture about it."

I gave Czech a look like, *Don't mind him.* But he raised up his glass anyway. "To the war," he toasted. "And all things fair and not fair."

"To the war!" Uncle Leo shouted. "To Gregory Peck and to General MacArthur. If only we'd let him nuke those commie bastards when we had the chance!"

"Yeah," I said, tipping my beer bottle. "The war. MacArthur. Nuclear proliferation." I didn't have the heart to tell Uncle Leo that Gregory Peck was a lifelong pacifist.

Taking a deep drink, I shifted my eyes back to Czech as he filled out my retainer check.

"So you decided to take the case," Lola says, as she pulls up outside of Georgie Phillips's townhouse, killing the engine. "For money, or out of curiosity?"

"A little of both," I say, pressing that blood-soaked towel tighter still against my side. "Even if I am convinced the guy is dead...long dead. If he isn't the Harvey Rose listed as alive, I have no doubt he's the dead guy. It's just that the poor Mr. Czech needs to be convinced of it. I hate to take his money just to hand him bad news, but if he wants to pay me, well then..."

"You cashed his check?"

"Cleared the next day."

Lola looks upset. Not upset over my ditching the hospital. But over something else. Like I've touched a nerve with the Czech story. Only I can't imagine how.

"You don't think I should have taken the gig or his money, Lo?"

She pulls the key from the starter.

"It's just that you have the bar now. You make OK money. Or, you will make OK money once business picks up, anyway. Why do you need to do PI work?" She peers down at her lap. "It's dangerous, Richard."

So that's it, then. The danger element. Guns and bad guys. Three toughies in Obama masks holding synthesizers to their throats, kicking the living snot out of me, leaving me for dead inside a back alley. Next time I'll be waiting for them along with my two good buddies, Smith and Wesson. I want to tell her this. But I know I can't.

"We have to go in," I say, "before I bleed to death."

Lola smiles, runs her hand over my nearly bald scalp. "No one can kill you, Richard," she says, "except yourself."

She gets out, starts up the walk toward Georgie's front door. While she walks I can't help but notice her perfect, valentine-shaped ass. Just the sight of it takes my breath away. Then I picture Some Young Guy's hand cupping it.

The remembered sight of that makes my blood boil.

What blood I have left over, that is.

CHAPTER 8

Back when I was a boy in Catholic grade school, the nuns used to conduct air raid drills once a month. It was the time of Red Scares and mutually assured nuclear destruction. And it scared the living daylights out of me.

The war against communist aggression in Vietnam was winding down, but that didn't prevent the major news networks from broadcasting video footage of our GIs being blown to smithereens on a daily basis. Films of napalm-spewing jets scorching the green jungle and, along with it, the Cong. Full-color video feeds of whole villages being torched; video of little girls running down the road, the clothing burned off their backs. Walter Cronkite telling the world the war is lost. President Johnson wailing, "Once we've lost Cronkite, we've lost the American people!"

We were fighting there in order to stop the spread of communism but losing badly. Because, after all, we were fighting the war with one hand tied behind our backs, the entire USA hippie contingent screaming about revolution and ending the madness.

"Give peace a chance!" Or fucking die!

But that still didn't stop the nuns in my school from convincing us that not only were the communists our enemy, but that they were out to nuke us first chance they got. The Russians worked for the devil. The Russians rejected Jesus. Thus the once-a-month duck-and-cover drills, where we stupidly assumed that by hiding under our school desks, our heads stuffed between our legs, we could somehow avoid total vaporization from a detonated nuclear bomb.

Place your heads between your thighs, kids, and kiss your asses good-bye.

The spread of communism was the last thing on Georgie Phillips's mind when he volunteered to kill commies on behalf of Uncle Sam. He'd been busy honing a teenage career of grand theft auto when the law finally caught up with him and a judge gave him a choice: five-to-seven in a maximum security prison or volunteer for the war. Since Georgie found the thought of crawling through the jungle and firing off machine guns much more appealing than getting bent over inside a prison shower, he immediately, quote, "volunteered," unquote. But what he saw over there and the things he was made to do in the name of democracy would have a dramatic effect on his life, not the least of which was eliminating his desire to jack any more cars. In fact, when he was discharged, Georgie used all of his GI bill to finish college and then entered med school.

For Georgie, the system of crime and punishment in a free America had worked.

That's when I first met the young man who would eventually become the big brother I never had.

He'd answered an ad my dad put in the local paper for a helper at the Moonlight Funeral Home. You know, somebody to help with the stiffs he'd drag down into the basement embalming room, somebody to pick them up from the morgue, someone to assist with the funerals both inside the parlor and inside

the church, and later at the cemetery. For a would-be pathologist, it was the perfect part-time gig.

Georgie's motto then and now is "lean and fucking mean."
Meaning he still can't weigh in at more than a buck-seventy
soaking wet. But between his wiry build and six-foot frame,
he's not only one of the strongest men, pound for pound, I've
ever known, he also possesses the endurance of a desert camel,
even after a protracted bout with skin cancer. And he loved his
work. Back in the day, he was such a good worker, he didn't
mind when families requested that the already-buried bodies
of loved ones be disinterred. It was a dirty job that required as
much muscle as it did skill, and I often acted as Georgie's sec-
ond-in-command when I approached my teenage years. In fact,
for Georgie, digging up a casket during the nighttime hours
was about as much fun as you could have with your clothes on,
especially when you brought along a case of beer or broke out a
big fat bomber of a spliff.

Maybe those were the good old days, and even though the
communist threat is all but a memory and our asses are still
intact, one thing remains true: Georgie still loves his weed. But
the ongoing brain bud love affair no longer has anything to do
with getting "high, high, high, in the midday sun." His painful
on-again, off-again battle with melanoma makes pot smoking a
medical necessity.

And the condition has assured him some of the best medi-
cally approved brain bud around, which he is now rolling into one
of his famous fatties. Meanwhile, I take a place of honor on the
stainless-steel table he's got set up in his basement lab, while the
suddenly squeamish Lola waits for us upstairs in the living room.

Since Georgie is retired from the official pathology business and now spends his time working on private medical

malpractice lawsuit cases for clients (mostly lawyers) who prefer to remain anonymous in exchange for cash-under-the-gurney projects, he doesn't bother with the formality of scrubbing up in green overalls and bibs. But he does wear latex gloves when he rubs Betadine solution all over the reopened laceration on my right side, and injects me with enough lidocaine to make my entire torso feel like it no longer exists.

"Can you tell me what the hell is going on?" Georgie says, his long gray hair tied back into a tight ponytail, his ears sporting real diamond stud pieces, each pulled from his two ex-wives' engagement rings after they threw them at him. Georgie never was the marrying kind.

I proceed to tell him the story of the three strangely voiced, Obama-masked thugs who killed me in the downtown back alley. Which leads me to something else.

"Georgie," I say, in between the painless but still pin-poking-through-foam-rubber sensation of a needle and thread entering and exiting my skin, "do you believe in life after death?"

The retired pathologist impales me with the final stitch, knots the thread, and cuts off the excess with a pair of stainless-steel scissors that he then tosses into a stainless-steel bowl. He takes some time to think about it while lighting up the new, medicinal-pot-filled fattie. Then he sucks in a huge hit of smoke and says, narrow-voiced, "I think all things are possible, especially when it comes to death." Releasing some of the pot smoke through his nostrils, he politely holds the joint out for me. Like always, I decline. Politely. "Little known fact about death: there are different levels. Lots of people die, in the clinical sense of no brain and heart function, but then get revived and have absolutely zero recollection of the experience. Those are the ones we never hear about, because their experience reflects the possibility of nothing after we cash it all in. How did Hemingway put it? 'Our Father who art in Nada.'

"But then again, I believe that the body contains an energy in the form of metabolism that some people call 'the soul.' " Now releasing the rest of the smoke, his voice returning to normal. "Doesn't matter what you call it. It's an energy that can be measured, and energy doesn't disappear; it merely becomes transformed. So in that sense, yeah, there's some kind of life after death."

"I saw things when I was dead," I reveal.

He just looks at me. Blank stare.

"I mean it. I was floating over the whole room, Georgie, just like you see on TV. I could see myself dead in the bed. I could see Lola."

Georgie takes another toke, smiles. With each breath of medicinal weed his state of permanent pain eases up just enough to make life not only bearable again but a joy to experience.

"Lola was there for you. Warms the heart."

I lift myself from the table, straighten myself up, the blood rushing back into my legs.

"Easy, Moon," Georgie warns. "You're gonna be a little wobbly."

My head feels light, but I'm feeling no pain. "Yeah, Lola being there was heartwarming," I say. " 'Cept for one thing."

"Which is?"

"There was a man with her."

He shakes his head like he doesn't get it.

"You know, a man. Some Young Guy. A total stranger. He came into the room after I was, well, deceased. He put his hand on her ass, Georgie."

Another toke off the joint. Harder this time. "Wait," he says and exhales, "let me get this straight. You're dead. Your soul is floating over your body, and it has eyes. You see your girlfriend standing by your corpse and suddenly some dude enters the picture and starts playing grab-ass with her."

"Yeah, something like that."

He starts to laugh.

"What's so funny?"

"First of all, Moon, even if it were really possible to see yourself dead, I doubt you'd be seeing reality. If you were experiencing anything it was probably some kind of whacked-out dream that occurred as the electrical system in your brain started to fade out, which thank God it didn't entirely do or you'd either be dead right now, or at the very least brain dead."

I feel suddenly lighter inside as opposed to light-headed, like maybe Some Young Guy really is a figment of my neurotic imagination. "You think I was making the dude up?"

"Moon, what kind of broad would be so heartless as to bring her new boyfriend to your deathbed? Unless..." He pauses midsentence, purses his lips. I hate it when Georgie pauses midsentence.

"Unless what, Georgie?"

He shakes his head, licks the pad of his index finger, pats out the joint. Then he turns his back on me, steps over to the counter, tosses the half-smoked joint into an empty Maxwell House coffee can, seals it with the plastic lid.

"Come on! Unless what?"

He turns back to me, a curious expression painting his face. "Unless she wanted to prove to the new squeeze that you were, in fact, a dead man."

OK, so Georgie's comment about proving my death to Some Young Guy smacks me upside the head. But then in the next sentence he tries to convince me that we're making mountains out of mud puddles and that the best thing to do is to simply forget about the whole thing and move on with my life. As shattered, fragile, and just plain messed up as it is.

I decide he's right, and as I'm slipping back into my bloodstained jeans as carefully as I can manage, I bring up the subject of Peter Czech. About the missing father, and the three Obama-masked thugs. I ask Georgie his opinion. Do I continue with the case? Or ditch it in the interest of preserving what life I have left? Or do I take a third course of action and go straight to the cops? Spill everything I know to Detective Clyne?

"This guy Czech," he says. "What's he paying you?"

I tell him. I also tell him that even though I cashed the check, I haven't started working on anything yet. Which makes my beating and subsequent murder all the more frustrating.

He purses his lips.

"Not bad dough. Sure you wanna give it up over three big bullies with weird voices?"

"They killed me once already, Georgie." Patting my now re-bandaged side. "And tortured me."

"Oh yeah, that. You've been picked on before. Never stopped you then. 'Sides, be nice to get some revenge, wouldn't it?"

He's got a point. I can get my hands on even one of those Obamas I'll kick the living snot out of him. But first things first. I dig out the photo Czech gave to me, hand it to Georgie. I point out the tall guy with the devil eyebrows as Czech's supposed biological father.

"I was hoping you could indulge my curiosity sweet tooth, big bro. I need to find out more info on contracted births and adoptions. How they work. If it's common for the now-adult kids to go looking for their biological parents."

"You weren't hired for that. Why waste your time?"

"You know how I am. I'm a worse snoop than my ex-wife. I wanna know the why behind the who in Czech's case."

He nods. "Fair enough," he says. "But how do you know if the birth was contracted by a surrogate mother?"

"Just a hunch, based on that photo. My built-in shit detector speaking to me. Why else would someone snap that picture of baby Peter with his new parents and his biological dad, but minus the mother?"

"Good point, Moon. Maybe she was simply too upset to go on record as having ditched the kid, even though she was just a kid herself. You're cooking with Wesson despite that head of yours."

"Gee, thanks. I also need to check into every accountant in Albany named Harvey Rose, maybe find an image and see if it even remotely matches Devil Brows."

"Sure he's still alive?" Georgie asks, eyes still fixed on the pic.

"Czech seems to think so, even if there is a Harvey Rose recorded as dead in the county records."

"Sounds pretty thin. Like he pulled the name from a phone book."

"Yeah, I get the same nagging pain in the gut, and it's got nothing to do with the incision or bruised kidneys. It tells me he's not really hiring me for what he says he's hiring me for."

Georgie tosses me a wink of his right eye. "You trying to hire me to assist you in this, ah, endeavor, Moon?"

"Mmm hmm."

"Sounds dangerous. Could get me into some serious trouble with some killer Obamas."

"Only the brave die noble."

"Who said that?"

"I think I made it up."

Moonlight the sage.

I slide off the table, picture Lola waiting for me upstairs in the living room of Georgie's townhouse. I know she's got her smartphone with her. I wonder if she's using it to text Some Young Guy. Or if, like Georgie suggested, dude's just a figment of my once-dying brain. I'm still not ready for the truth either way. What if my soul really does exist? What if it did reveal Lola's affair on its aborted road trip out of town? I've loved and lost once before to an affair, and it nearly killed me. Rather, *I* nearly killed me. I'm not sure how I'd react to another case of love gone sour over another man. But I know it wouldn't be good.

I hobble toward the door that leads to the staircase.

"You look into the contract baby-selling business," I say to Georgie. "Then meet me at my place later on tonight. Seven o'clock."

"What's the plan?"

"Surveillance mission."

"Lola?"

I shake my head. "Peter Czech."

"I'll bring coffee and sandwiches."

"I'll bring the binocs," I say, limping up the steps. Painfully.

"And why are we doing this?"

"I've got a bad feeling about Mr. Czech."

"When was the last time you felt good about anybody who hires Captain Head Case?"

CHAPTER 9

Lola is patiently waiting for me upstairs. I'm not usually the sneaky type, but even with the wound in my side and half my body numb, I try to step as lightly as possible, which isn't easy with my limp.

Maybe I'm being paranoid about nothing.

But then, maybe my built-in shit detector is trying to tell me something. As I slowly open the door to the living room, I can see through the crack that Lola is texting something into her cell. Frantically texting, opposing thumbs bouncing off the keypad. When I open the door all the way and limp out, she quickly stuffs the phone back into her bag, plants a smile on her face.

"How is it?" she asks, referring to my newly sutured side.

Her hands are trembling. I look at them. She looks at me looking at them. We don't speak about our noticing the same things. But it's like we're shouting at one another.

"No more bleeding. But it's gonna be painful later on."

She stands up, the strap on her bag hanging off her shoulder. I hear a distinct chime coming from inside it.

"Sounds like you just got a text."

She nods, eyes wide. Her hands go from trembling to outright shaking.

"Go ahead and read it, Lo."

If she were in possession of an Adam's apple, it would be jumping up and down in her neck along with her shaking hands. "We need to get you home," she says through clenched teeth.

"Yeah," I say, my right hand pressed against my side. "I should get home."

Turning, I head for the front door, knowing in my bones that Lola is hiding something from me, and that it quite possibly has everything to do with the man I saw embracing her over my corpse.

CHAPTER 10

Pulling up in front of my new Hudson riverside loft, which is situated inside the now deserted Port of Albany, Lola kills the Hummer engine like she's about to come inside with me. She almost always comes inside with me.

"I can handle it from here," I say. But I'm lying. It isn't the truth. If I were being honest I would tell her that I'm exhausted, in pain, and not sure I'm thinking all too clearly. But I know that Lola's hiding something, and it makes me want to run away, not have her in for a sleepover.

I open the door. She reaches out for me, takes hold of my arm.

"Richard," she says, tightening her grip on my forearm. But instead of saying anything else, she just clams up, her grip tight on my arm. "Richard, I..."

"What is it?"

But her lips are sewn shut. Until she says, "I want you to consider not going ahead with this Peter Czech thing."

What the hell is happening here? First three masked men beat me senseless over my new client, and now Lola is getting in on the action.

"Lola, what are you trying to tell me?"

She bites down hard on her lip. "I don't have a good feeling about it. Look at what's already happened."

I feel the pressure of the stitches on my side as the lidocaine begins to wear off. "I've never backed down from a gig before, Lo. And I'm not about to start. Besides, Czech has his claws buried in me now. And I also want to find out who those masked bastards are, why they killed me once already, why they want me to drop my client, and last but most certainly not least, what the contents are of this box I'm supposed to possess."

She releases her grip on my arm. "No talking you out of it, huh?"

"It got entirely personal when they tried to kill me."

She nods, starts the Hummer back up. I open the door, slip on out, stand facing her.

She adds, "You might not like what you find out about Czech, Moon."

"OK, what is it you're not telling me, Lo?" How many versions of the same question can I possibly lob at her?

She throws the Hummer in drive. "Just close the door," she insists, a single tear rolling down her cheek. A single tear filled with anger, sadness, fear, and frustration.

"Lola, come on...What's happening? Do you know Czech?"

"Close. The. Door."

"Will I hear from you later?"

"I don't think so. Close it. Now. Please."

I close it.

The slam reverberates over the old docks and the slow-moving river. It's as lonely as a ship's bell softly clanging somewhere off in a thick foggy distance.

The Hummer engine revs.

Lola splits.

CHAPTER 11

I crawl into the loft, waddle over to my futon, collapse onto it, fall immediately to sleep.

In the dream you're once more floating over your body. Only this time you're not inside the hospital room. You're inside Lola's bedroom. She's lying naked on the bed, faceup. Both her arms are tied to opposing bedposts, as are her legs.

There are three people surrounding her bed.

One on each side and one at the foot. They're dressed in black, wearing Obama masks. All three of them have those electronic voice synthesizers pressed up under their jaws. They're not saying anything. They're just humming in unison, the noise growing louder and louder, agitating Lola with each rise in decibel until she's thrusting out her hips and pulling on the ropes. From your perch above her you want to dive down and help her. Only you can't do it. You're stuck up there at the ceiling.

And then a third person enters the room. It's a man. It's Some Young Guy. Rather, it's faceless Some Young Guy. Or, what serves as his face has been blocked out or distorted like they do on those true crime shows when they arrest some drunk driver who insists that his face not be shown on TV. The Obama at the end of the bed makes room for him. Faceless Some Young Guy undresses, gets on top of Lola, enters her.

They do it just like that on the bed to the electronic soundtrack of those artificial voice boxes. Until finally Lola screams in climax and you...

...wake up.

Darkness fills the first-floor loft space.

How long was I asleep. An hour? Three? It had to be at least three. I look at my wristwatch. Fifteen past five. I've slept for over three hours. I slide off the bed, more than a bit groggy. There's some blood smeared on the bed sheet from where I rolled over onto my right side. I touch my shirt and find that it's wet. I turn on the lamp, pull off the shirt and the old dressing, check the wound in the mirror above the dresser. The stitches seem intact, but the blood is still leaking through. I put on fresh dressing and a clean shirt. I've slept long enough. Time to get to work once and for all on the Peter Czech case. Find out if he is who he says he is, and if he is in fact looking for a man who he swears is his biological father.

I'd start on the project immediately too, if not for the figure of a man standing in the shadows.

CHAPTER 12

"Sorry if I startled you," says trench-coated Detective Clyne. "The door. It was open."

My heart dislodges itself from my throat, slowly drops back down into my bruised rib cage. He's right. I rarely lock it. It's a big industrial wood slider that's secured with a padlock. Sometimes I'm lazy about it.

"You're the cops," I say and exhale.

"What's that got to do with it?"

"Being a cop means never having to say you're sorry."

He smiles that sad smile of his and steps into the inverted cone of white overhead light. The kind of white light that shines down from one of those ceiling-mounted warehouse lamps.

"Whaddya got to drink around this place?" he asks, scoping the wide-open loft with deep-set brown eyes. Tired eyes.

"I've got a bottle or two. You here on official business, Clyne? Or did you miss me?"

"Let's get that drink," he says, and together we settle in on the barstools set in front of the island counter that serves as my kitchen.

"To answer your question," Clyne says over a clear drinking glass with a double shot of Jack in it, "I went to the hospital, and they said you discharged yourself. I didn't believe them. Considering the shape you were in."

"It's the truth," I insist, though I suppose he doesn't necessarily need convincing, seeing as how I'm sitting here right in front of him.

He takes a sip of the whiskey, lets it settle on his tongue, then swallows thoughtfully. "Pretty risky for a guy who technically bought the farm just the other day."

"It was either bolt or die...on a permanent basis."

"They came back for you, didn't they? Sometime around nine in the morning. Or so I'm told."

In my mind I picture the little blond nurse who tried to stop me from leaving. She must have told him everything.

"I don't recall the time." I take a sip of my own glass of Jack. A glass that holds only a single shot. I wouldn't want to alarm the dick by overdoing my booze privileges so soon after my resurrection.

"You should have called me right away."

"Yup."

"You gonna start that 'yup' thing?"

"Nope."

He makes a corner-of-the-mouth smirk. "Look, Moonlight, it's been a long day so far, and I'd really like to get home and put up my dogs and get drunk in peace, so if you could spare the ball busting."

I take another drink, nod. I'm too beat up to keep giving him a hard time. "Three of them this time. Same three, I'm guessing, wearing those silly Obama masks and using the voice synthesizers."

He pulls that same small spiral notebook from the interior of his trench coat, jots down a note. "How'd they get in, you think?"

"You're asking me?"

"Yup." He smiles. Drinks the rest of his whiskey. I pour him another.

"OK, Clyne. My guess is it's possible they know someone in the hospital. That's my theory anyway, as a former cop."

"And brilliant private dick," he adds.

"Who's busting balls now?" I laugh and hold up my whiskey glass for him to clink. Which he does. Good to have a new friend among my APD enemies.

"What did they want this time?"

"Other than to torture me by pulling out one of my staples, they switched the focus of their warnings from staying away from Peter Czech to something else. They want a box of some kind."

"What box?"

"That's the eternal question. Apparently Czech came to visit me, which I most definitely don't remember, and he was supposed to have given me some kind of box with something in it. Now these Obamas are convinced I have the box and they want it too."

He drinks some more Jack, gazes at me quizzically. How would Agatha Christie put it? Gazes at me...*rather quizzically*.

"So what's in the box?"

"Clyne, I just told you I have no memory of the box. So how could I possibly know what's in it?"

"Good retort. Allow me to rephrase. What, in your expert opinion, Mr. Moonlight, could be contained in this box the masked fellows who caved your face in want?"

I cock my head and feel an itchy pain in my side where Georgie sewed me up. The lidocaine is really wearing off now. "Not a fucking clue."

"But it's got to be worth a pretty penny. Or these people wouldn't be willing to kill and torture to get at it."

"Agreed."

"And they're convinced Czech left it for you, and you just don't recall because of your..." He makes like a pistol and points to his head.

"My accident," I say. But we both know that the words he's avoiding are "attempted suicide."

We both sit in pregnant silence for a minute, until he downs the rest of his booze and I do the same.

He gets up.

I go to get up too.

"Don't bother," he says, aiming his eyes at my side and the small blotch of blood that now stains my shirt. "That must smart."

"Smart never seems to enter into my vocabulary, Clyne. No matter the connotation."

"Something like this happens again, you'll call me, right?"

"Yup."

"And should you happen to locate this, uh, box, you'll pick up the phone?"

"Most definitely."

"Because you never know what can be in this box, what importance or danger lurks inside it. So my advice to you is to stay away from it, should it show up. Simply call me, day or dark of night. I'll take it from there."

"Most definitely, Detective Clyne." I hold my right hand up, two fingers raised high in the Boy Scout salute. Christ, it hurts even to hold my fingers up.

He stands there, big and sad and lonely and draped in a tan trench coat. The look in his eyes...It's like he's staring at a corpse waiting to happen. And he is.

Turning for the door, he lets himself out without thanking me for the drinks or saying good-bye. A true Albany cop if I ever saw one.

CHAPTER 13

Yet another new shirt on, along with a tighter bandage, I've got the Dell laptop open on the kitchen island. I've switched to beer, an economy-sized Bud tallboy positioned next to the computer for easy access. Thank God for wireless Internet. Allows me to multitask.

Planted on the barstool, I go onto Google, type the name "Peter Czech" into the search engine, press Enter. Not a damn thing comes up. Nothing about him belonging to a professional society of nuclear engineers, nothing regarding high school or college alumni. No Facebook page or Twitter account. As far as the Internet and social media are concerned, Czech is anonymous. And considering he works for a facility that deals on a daily basis with classified nuclear information, maybe that's to be expected.

I sit back, take a sip of beer.

Even though the bleeding has stopped, the pain in my side is getting worse. I tap the bandaged wound gently with my fingers. It sends a small shockwave of sting up and down my side.

Lidocaine officially worn off.

I get up, find the Advils on the metal shelf mounted above the sink, pour four into my hand. Sitting back down at the counter, I swallow all four not with tap water but with a swig of beer. Pays to live dangerously.

Next search: Harvey Rose.

I get the Web site for the New York State Society for CPAs. Now there's some excitement. I type "Harvey Rose" into the site-specific search engine and receive only a single business address that's located downtown on State Street. Not far from the alley where those three thugs beat the snot out of me. I write the address down on a piece of scrap paper, stuff it into my pocket. Later on, after Georgie gets here, I'll attempt to pay a visit to Mr. Rose's office, see if he does in fact look like the man in Czech's black-and-white photo, only thirty-plus years older.

Next item: I search for the online version of the Albany County Hall of Records. When it comes up, I make a site search for "Harvey Rose." Sure enough, just like Czech said, one Harvey Rose pops up. No information, other than his being listed as "deceased." Under occupation it says "businessman." No next of kin, no cemetery address, no contact information for surviving family, not even a birth or death date.

I click off the site.

Final item of business. Maybe there's nothing noteworthy about Czech on the Web, but I can bet my remaining days he's located in the WhitePages.com. And that's the way it turns out. He lives in a North Albany suburb called Loudonville. Four Orchard Grove, just like he revealed during our first meeting together at my bar. It's exactly where I will be heading tonight, soon as Georgie gets here.

CHAPTER 14

By eight o'clock, the pain in my side is beginning to subside. On that stupid one-to-ten pain scale the docs make you refer to, the sting is now reduced to a more comfortable six or seven. The beers are helping. Which is why I decide to grab another cold one from the fridge. I pop the cap, take a swig. My cell vibrates. I pull it out of my pocket.

Text. From Lola.

She asks me how I'm feeling. I thumb a message back to her telling her I'm fine. Never better. It's a lie, of course. I'm dizzy, in pain, still bleeding, and drinking like a fish. I ask her if she wants me to come over.

"Now's not a good time," she texts.

She's never said that to me before.

I picture her lying naked in bed with Some Young Guy, tickling one another's feet under the covers with their big toes. I picture him doing all those things to her that I used to do, and it makes my stomach cramp up and throb with more pain than the gash in my side. On a scale of one to ten, the pain is an eleven.

I don't text her back after that.

I just drink.

Drink and ache.

CHAPTER 15

I sit for a while thinking things out.

I start from the start, from the moment Czech first met me at my bar in his wheelchair a few days ago. Moonlight FYI: whenever anyone hires me for something, I can't help but wonder why. Why hire a guy with half a bullet in his brain and a penchant for forgetting things when you can hire a perfectly normal person?

Maybe I just come cheap. Maybe that's what it comes down to: price. These are tough times, after all. Four bucks a gallon for gas, three bucks for a loaf of bread, most of a twenty-dollar bill for a six-pack of brew and a single pack of Marlboros. Tough times even for nuclear engineers.

I take a sip of beer, sit back, and think about all that I have to go on. First things first: I have a handicapped guy who wants me to find his long-lost biological father. I've got a three-decade-old photograph of said father standing beside a pair of adoptive parents named Czech who originally migrated from the then USSR, only to settle in Albany to start a new life for themselves. That new life afforded Papa Czech employment as an engineer at the Knolls nuclear power plant. It would eventually include his son's employment as well. And, for an added connection, the son's biological father belongs to a team of accountants who oversaw the plant on behalf of the federal government.

Not six degrees of separation. Just three.

Speaking of the biological father: he's tall and bears eyebrows so thick and long they curl up at the end, making him look a lot like a cartoon devil. After thirty years, I picture the eyebrows having turned gray and perhaps having even grown out all the more.

The point is, if Harvey Rose still exists, he will not be hard to spot. Unless he trims his brows regularly.

And since the business address of one Harvey Rose exists in the Google business listings, there's nothing preventing me from driving over to his office and knocking on the door. Problem is, Peter Czech has already told me that if finding his old man was as easy as going online, he wouldn't have needed me in the first place.

Am I to assume then that the Rose I've just discovered at work on State Street is not Czech's father? Maybe. But it still won't hurt to check out the office. Pays to be thorough. Or maybe Czech's gut instinct is all wrong and Rose is in fact the dead guy listed in the Albany County Hall of Records.

All things considered, Czech's father-finding project should not be all that difficult if all I have to do is some digging around. I'll eventually find the man if he's alive. And I'll find him if he's dead. Problem is, I've got three Obama-masked men dressed in black who've threatened to kill me if I keep on looking for Czech's biological father. Now they not only want to kill me, but they want the contents of some box Czech apparently brought to my bedside in the Albany Medical Center—a transaction he denies, and of which I have no recollection.

Go figure.

To make matters worse, my longtime girlfriend, Lola, is begging me not to take Czech's job, like she too knows something I don't.

Have I truly seen her with another man standing beside my deathbed only two days ago? If I believe Georgie, then what I witnessed could very well be an elaborate dream. But I'm not so sure it's a dream. Lola is acting way too strange, too secretive. Like she's indeed conducting an affair behind my back.

There's something else gnawing at my brain too. Maybe I have no grounds on which to base my assumption. Or maybe I'm just plain crazy, a head case with a small piece of .22 caliber bullet inside his brain. But my built-in shit detector is sounding off again, and I somehow can't help but believe that Lola and Peter Czech know one another. And if that's the case, then the Lola I've known all this time isn't the woman she appears to be. It also means that Czech isn't the helpless handicapped client I've perceived him to be either.

It all adds up to mean that I'm being duped and have died once already in the process.

CHAPTER 16

My big bro shows up at my place at eight thirty.

Time enough for us to down a couple more painkilling beers while we discuss his little research project regarding contract births. We sit at my kitchen counter while Georgie tells me that since back in the late seventies, women—especially, quote, "liberated," unquote, women—have been entering into contracts to carry and deliver perfectly healthy babies for couples who, for one reason or another, cannot have one. Maybe they're infertile, too old, or too gay.

Whatever the case, the "adoptive parents," as they came to be called, enter into a legally binding contract with the "host mother," as she's called, which dictates that immediately upon birth, custody of the child will revert to the adoptive mother and father. The child, it is understood, will never see his or her biological host mother again. Nor will there be contact.

That sad fact alone might explain the one known photograph that exists of baby Czech along with his new Russian parents, his biological father, but not his biological mother.

"The common problem that arises down the road," Georgie adds, "is that lots of biological mothers can't resist the temptation…hell, the biological need…to try to get their kids back. Or at least make contact with them. Same goes for the kids wanting to see their real parents, which could be the case with your client. That is, if you're looking for a motivation here, which I assume you are."

"I suppose. You can't deny hundreds of thousands of years of human genetic makeup," I suggest. "It's just not a natural act for a woman to willingly give up a baby she carried for nine months inside her own womb. Her own flesh and blood."

I pull out the strange photo of baby Peter Czech, his adoptive parents, and his biological father. There's no joy in the eyes of the new parents, and nothing but a kind of grim satisfaction in the biological dad's. That's when it hits me: "Unless the biological mother was forced into giving up her child against her will."

"I don't follow," Georgie says.

"Unless someone didn't want her having the child," I say. "Like her husband perhaps. An *angry* husband or boyfriend."

"Maybe angry because the child wasn't his to begin with," Georgie says, our minds working the angle together now.

I nod, pull the black-and-white photo close, like maybe staring at it some more will offer more clues.

"Could be that what we're witnessing inside this photo, Georgie, is a man who really isn't Peter's father at all, but some guy who's so pissed off at his wife for cheating on him, he enters into a contract with a Russian couple to raise her illegitimate child."

"Cold," Georgie says. "And entirely fucked up."

"Très cold," I agree, getting up from the counter to fetch one last cold beer.

"Richard!" Georgie barks while I'm pulling the can from the fridge.

I turn fast. Georgie only calls me Richard when he's about to come down on me for something.

"What's with the damn drinking?"

"I'm in pain," I tell him. "Real. Physical. Pain." But he sees right through my fib.

"From your war wounds? Or from something else?"

Lola and Some Young Guy embracing over my dead body.

I turn back to the fridge, open it, slide the beer back inside.

"Let's just fucking go."

CHAPTER 17

Of course, all these assumptions are just that: assumptions.

I've still been hired to find old Devil Brows, no matter what the circumstances are behind Czech's adoption, and that's what I'm going to do.

Why am I such a nosy busybody?

Why am I always looking for answers to questions that don't really matter?

Because I want to know what and whom I'm dealing with. Which means parking myself outside Czech's home for a few hours.

Moonlight the thorough.

Inside the bedroom area of the loft, I find my .9 mm hanging on the bedpost by its leather shoulder holster. I strap it on outside my black turtleneck. In the drawer I find my Swiss Army knife and stuff that into the right-hand pocket of my black Levi's. After I step into some lace-up combat boots, I slip on my leather jacket, button it up. For a final touch, a black wool watch cap from the army/navy. All I need now is a thin mustache and I'll be David Niven in *The Guns of Navarone*.

Out in the hallway, Georgie and I take a quick glance at one another. We're both dressed entirely in black denim and leather. This is hardly our first stakeout, and by now we know the drill.

Besides, we both look good in black.

We don't head immediately to Czech's house.

At my insistence, we make a detour first via downtown Albany. State Street, to be precise. The uphill city street that Teddy Roosevelt climbed every day to the state capitol back in the old days when the potbellied, moustached Rough Rider was the governor of New York State and dying of cabin fever.

Georgie drives the van slowly, the flashers going so that the crappy drivers glued to our ass end know enough to pull around us. Meanwhile, we search for the number 45 planted on one of the glass-and-metal entries to the old brick high-rises.

I spot 45, tell him to stop.

He pulls over, double parks beside a white van that has the words "Capital Cleaning Crew" printed on the side panels.

"Be right back," I say, getting out. "Cop comes, just drive around the block."

I approach the entrance to 45 State Street. Even though it's after business hours, the door is open. To my immediate left inside the wide-open marble-finished vestibule is a building directory. I pull the small piece of scrap paper from my pocket, look at it.

Harvey Rose, CPA
45 State Street
Suite 12B
Albany, New York

"X marks the fucking spot," I whisper to myself, while a two-man cleaning crew goes to work buffing the floors with big, electric-powered buffers. The Capital Cleaning Crew no doubt.

I stare up at the board, hoping the cleaning crew won't expect the worst from a grown man dressed all in black sneaking inside a commercial building after business hours. First I look for a name: Rose. When the name doesn't appear, I look for the suite number: 12B. The suite number is there. But no Rose. Instead it says "Dental Office."

Being a clever, tenacious, and recently mortally wounded private detective, I decide to make an on-the-spot investigation.

When the cleaning crew isn't looking, I slip into the stairwell, make my way up one flight of stairs. Then I exit the stairwell and find the elevator. I take it to the twelfth floor. I make my way down a dimly lit, carpeted hall, until I come to suite 12B. The name on the door doesn't resemble Rose's one bit. In fact, it isn't even an accounting firm. Like the directory indicates, the door says "Dr. Thomas Doolittle, Dentist."

Dr. Doolittle. I wonder if he works only on animals, seeing as only he can speak to them.

After a quick but exhaustive check of every office on the floor, I take the elevator back down to the first floor. When the doors open, an agitated man in a business suit holding a brown leather attaché case gets on. As I get off, I about-face.

"Excuse me, sir," I say. "Do you work in this building?"

His eyes blink rapidly. The doors start to close and he has no choice but to hold them open. I take a step forward, place my booted foot in front of the left door, just in case he has trouble holding it.

"Yes," he says.

"How many years?"

He exhales. He wants to go upstairs in the worst way. He looks down at my foot in the door, up at me. "About a dozen. Why? Can I help you with something?"

"I'm looking for Harvey Rose, CPA. I have a card says he works here on the twelfth floor."

He shakes his head, purses his lips. "That agency hasn't been around for at least five years," he explains. "That it? I answer your question?"

Just then a young redheaded woman enters the building, makes her way to the elevator. She's startled to see the man holding the door open. "Brian," she says and exhales, nervously, as she steps inside.

She's dressed in a short skirt, white blouse unbuttoned enough to show some cleavage. Her jacket matches her skirt. She's got a diamond-mounted silver band wrapped around her wedding finger. Expensive.

"Audrey," he mumbles. "Nice to...see you." Brian's face turns red, like his friend's hair. He tries to put on a good act, but he isn't much of a faker. When I step back, I notice that Brian wears a wedding band himself. Gold. Inexpensive.

"Burning the midnight oil, Brian?" I say. I just can't resist. Moonlight the ballbuster.

The elevator doors close before he can respond. Just as well.

As I make for the exit past the busy-at-work Capital Cleaning Crew, I'm reminded of Some Young Guy, of Lola, of my ex-wife.

I'm also reminded of how much I hate cheaters.

CHAPTER 18

I slip back into the van.

Georgie peers at me with those deep blue eyes. "I'm guessing we've reached a crucial plot point in the mystery. Let me guess: no Rose."

"The address is old. I'm surprised it's listed on Google at all."

"Maybe someone *wants* it on Google. You gotta feed that search engine bitch before it will tag something. And Rose's address has apparently been tagged, even if it is a phony. I mean, I can't be sure, Moon, but that's the way it appears to me."

"The only thing for certain is the pain in my side and the constant ringing in my skull."

"Poor baby."

"When you gonna stop picking on me?"

He throws the tranny into drive. "On the last day of never," he says.

"Drive," I say.

"Yes, sir, sir," he says.

CHAPTER 19

About a half hour later, Georgie and I are parked across the street and down a ways from Czech's Orchard Grove crib. The place is a featureless, just-add-water, single-story ranch. It looks identical to the thousand-plus others that surround it in a quiet neighborhood that appears to have sprung up immediately after World War II. That sleepiness means it won't be long before someone calls the cops on Georgie's F5 Ford extended van. Which makes it all the more important that I try to catch sight of Czech sooner rather than later, see if there's anything about him that appears to be different from the young man he portrays himself to be.

Thus far, however, it doesn't look like he's home.

We wait another hour, with the occasional car passing us, the driver almost always slowing up to get a good look at the two men dressed in black and parked on the side of the road opposite Czech's. For all I know, the neighborhood watch committee is already on to us.

"Time to take a drive-around, Georgie," I suggest, after a time.

"Sure about that?" He sips on coffee kept warm in his thermos.

"It's either that or have the APD pull up on our asses."

I recall Detective Clyne's business card still stuffed inside my pants pocket. Should I call him, alert him to what we're up to? Better not to open that Pandora's box.

Georgie slips the coffee into one of the console cup holders, turns over the engine. "I hear you, Moon," he says. "Just a quick drive around the block. Break things up."

It's exactly what we do.

When we get back, Czech's house is still draped in blackness. Some of the other surrounding homes have also gone black. It's after ten o'clock at night. I can't be sure if people go to sleep before the eleven o'clock news in this neighborhood, or if they're all getting a good look at us through their living room picture windows.

Flashlight.

A circle of blinding white light.

"Oh crap." Georgie, barking under his breath.

"Be cool. And pull that rubber band out of your hair."

Shooting me a look.

"Just do it, G."

He does it.

"Come close," I insist.

"Moon—"

"Georgie, we are not going to be reported to the cops."

He scooches closer. That's when I grab him by the shoulders, pull him into me, run my hands through his long, shoulder-length hair, and lay a big fat kiss on him. No tongue, of course.

A tap on the driver's-side window behind Georgie.

"What the fuck!" Georgie pulls back. I think he's going to spit in my face.

"Don't turn around, or this is shot."

Another rap on the glass, the flashlight lighting up the cab. I reach out around Georgie, roll down the window.

"Excuse me," a balding middle-aged man says. "But this is a private neighborhood, and we strongly discourage people from using it for illicit purposes."

I work up my best Moonlight smile. "You mean like making out?"

"Whatever," the man says.

"Listen, buddy, I completely understand. I live in a suburb myself across the river in Troy. But my girlfriend here is upset. She's here visiting her parents, and we were just grabbing a minute to talk in peace. So just give us a few minutes and we'll be on our merry way."

The man shines the light on Georgie's long gray hair. "Her parents must be pretty old. What are their names? I'm sure I must know them."

My smile dissolves. "Here's an idea, pal. Maybe dispense with hurtful remarks, OK? My girlfriend happens to be prematurely gray, and I happen to think it's beautiful."

He pulls the light away. "I'm sorry," he offers. "I didn't mean any disrespect. And it *is* lovely. Who did you say her parents are?"

"I didn't."

"Miss?" the man pushes. "Would you mind telling me who your parents are so I can alert our friendly neighborhood watch committee?"

Georgie straightens up but keeps his back to the man. "Please just leave us alone!" he screams in a voice that sounds like I've just grabbed hold of his nuts. Then he buries his face in his hands.

"Now look what you've done!" I snap.

The man backs away, rattled. "Listen," he says, "my bad. Take the time you need. Sorry if I bothered—"

"We'll be gone in a few minutes," I say, then reach back around Georgie to crank the window closed.

Middle-Aged Man walks away, fading back into the night.

Georgie shoots back over to the other side of the van.

"Kiss me again," he hisses, "and you die for real."

CHAPTER 20

Night drags on.

As convincing as our boyfriend-upset-girlfriend act might have been, the time is closing in on midnight. I know it won't be long until the real cops arrive. But then two halogen headlights break through the darkness. They belong to a four-door sedan that passes us by and pulls into Czech's driveway.

Score.

Czech guns the car up the driveway incline. At first I think he might plow right through the garage door. But then he hits the brakes only a foot or so from the door, the boat of a modified car rocking and bouncing on bad shocks, just like my dad's old black Cadillac hearse. The headlamps shine bright on the overhead garage door, until the door suddenly starts raising up and the light fills the garage interior.

The car jolts forward once more and then skids to a stop inside the garage.

"Your client likes his cocktails," Georgie chuckles.

"Go easy on him. He's handicapped...I think."

By now I have my binoculars out. They aren't equipped with night vision like you see in the movies. But they are UV coated. I purchased them on clearance for fifteen bucks at my local drugstore. With the garage light on, I have no trouble making Czech out. I see him swing his legs out and plant his feet firmly on the floor of the garage. Then he reaches into the backseat, opens the back door. It opens in the opposite manner a door will usually open, the hinges mounted toward the trunk rather than at the midpoint of the cab. The same way the doors work on an old-fashioned limo. Like the kind my dad used to hire out on occasion for a client willing to pay up for the A-level funeral procession package. A custom body job no doubt designed specially for his handicap.

I see him reaching for something, which I assume is a wheelchair. When he pulls himself out of the car by his arms and sits down hard into something, I know I'm right. He closes the driver's-side door, then closes the back door, and begins to wheel himself around the back side of the car.

I keep my binocs on him the entire time. When he stops about midway across the back of the car and spots the van, I can't help but think that he's spotted me too. His employer spying on him. Even from that distance I can feel him looking right into my eyes, as if he can somehow make up for his paralyzed condition with superhuman eyesight.

"Start the van, Georgie. But leave the lights off."

Georgie starts it. Czech turns back to the garage, wheels himself inside. The garage door comes down. Maybe ten or fifteen seconds later, the lights go on in the house. I aim the spyglasses at the living room window, which is covered in drapes. When I see them open just a crack, I know Czech is eyeing us again.

"Let's go," I suggest.

My girlfriend Georgie drives.

CHAPTER 21

We're driving back toward my loft.

"So tell me, Moon," Georgie says after a time. "What was the point of that little exercise?"

"You gotta ask?"

He turns to me while driving, that long gray-white hair still draping his face like a guitar dude from ZZ Top, sans the Santa beard.

"You thought he was faking his paralysis, didn't you?"

"Stranger things have happened."

"You don't trust your client." His right hand shoots up, index finger pointing at the van ceiling. "Correction, you *never* trust your clients."

"Jim Rockford's rule number one in the private detective's handbook: never trust your client, especially if she's a woman. Didn't you ever watch *The Rockford Files*?"

"You're dating yourself. And apparently for you and Jim Rockford, a handicapped person falls under the female category. What are you, a fucking caveman?"

"Jim Rockford's rule number two: never trust a handicapped client who can pound two pint-sized Jack and Cokes in about twenty minutes and still drive a straight line out of your drinking establishment."

"Hmmm," he mumbles, pulling up outside my two-story building. "Out of curiosity, what's Rockford's rule number three?"

He comes to a stop, kills the engine and the lights.

"Never trust a client who's willing to spend good money to hire a head case like me. That's actually my personal rule. Jim Rockford was worth the money. After all, we're talking James Garner here...in his prime."

"I'm in my prime, Moon. Even if I do feel old."

"This ain't about you. 'Sides, when it comes to that body of yours, it's the mileage, not the years. And you're still strong as an ox. Just a little worn around the treads."

I open my door. Georgie opens his.

I have no idea what hits me before my world turns black.

CHAPTER 22

Here's the deal: you're dead again.

Or, at least you're pretty sure you're dead. Because just like last time, you're floating over your body in the far corner of a room with no windows. Looks a lot like a basement with concrete walls and a concrete floor. In the background, a garden-variety Sears boiler and a hot-water tank with the ductwork and piping ripped out.

You're laid out on some sort of gurney or table. Duct tape covers your mouth. Your legs and arms are duct taped together at the wrists and ankles. In fact, your whole body is duct taped to the table. You can't move anymore. Not with the blood that covers your chest and neck. Not with the blood that's pouring off the table, pooling onto the concrete floor. Not with your heart no longer beating, your brain no longer functioning.

It's the same with Georgie.

He's been duct taped to a second table directly beside your own. While your eyes are closed, his are wide open, watching the three Obama-masked men in black poke him with something that looks like a hair dryer. Electrocuting him with wires that stick out of the nozzle.

Like you, Georgie's also bleeding from numerous lacerations and scrapes. As the electrical charges are applied, you can see him trying to back away. But there's nowhere to go. While the men standing on either side of him take turns doing the torturing, the third one stands at the foot of the table and presses that voice machine against his throat.

"Where is the zeepy box?" he demands in that foreign electronic voice. "Your partner...he has box, yes? We need box."

From where you're looking down on these three motherfuckers, you want to tell them you don't have their precious box...whatever the fuck a zeepy box is. That you never had a box. That you don't even remember looking at the box. That they have the wrong man. It's Czech they want. Not you. Not Georgie.

As much as it pains you to see Georgie being tortured for something that's your fault, you're feeling kind of glad that you're dead again. You're starting to like this out-of-body-no-pain thing. You're just waiting for the little speck of bright white light to reappear and for that roller coaster ride through the wormhole. You're looking forward to seeing the old man again. You'll miss Lola, but you're not sure she'll miss you. Not with Some Young Guy to keep her company now.

But then something happens.

You feel yourself drifting. Only not in the right direction. You feel yourself drifting back down toward your bloody, beat-up, sweat-soaked body. It's slow at first, and you do your best to resist the movement south. But how can you resist when you are no longer flesh and blood?

It takes only a few seconds, and like a foot slipped into a well-worn boot, you're back in your body.

CHAPTER 23

OK, maybe I didn't die again, after all.

Maybe I was only dreaming. Maybe I was delusional after having been knocked unconscious for the second time in a few days, my already fragile brain screaming, *Uncle!*

When I open my eyes I feel more pain pressing up against my eyeballs than I can possibly comprehend. Imagine Conan the Barbarian shoving his sausage-thick thumbs into both your eye sockets until they pop out the back end of your skull. So much pain, I'm *wishing* myself dead. I know it's difficult to stay alive sometimes, but is it really that hard to fucking die?

Turning my head, I manage a quick glance over my shoulder.

Georgie's laid out on the table beside me. I try to scream through my duct-tape-covered mouth. Whatever I'm doing, it must be working. Because I manage to catch the attention of the Obama-masked leader, the one with the cancer machine now pressed up against his throat. He glances at me while the other two Obamas are busy applying those exposed electrical wires to Georgie's mams. While the bigger of the two Obamas holds my big brother down, the far smaller one keeps trying to shift the hair dryer from slow to rapid air, and at the same time increasing the electrical charge in the wires. Or so I assume.

But something seems to be the matter.

The hair dryer is plugged in, but it doesn't seem to be working, so they have to be content with sticking Georgie with the sharp ends of the wire.

"What kind of torture you think this is?" says the smaller Obama, revealing his voice without the synthesizer. Russian. The voice is most definitely Russian.

"I cannot work under such conditions," says the other. He's talking without his voice machine also. Another Russian. "In mother country, we can count on reliable Russian nuclear reactor to provide power. Here, in U-S-of-A, the fucking Bambi lovers won't have nuclear reactor. Except in bombs. America is soft and fat and stupid, yes?"

The smaller Obama keeps poking Georgie with the wires anyway. He keeps flicking the switch like he's convinced the power is about to come back on at any moment.

Georgie's face is beet red and tighter than a tick. I'm not sure how much pain he's in. But if they could tap the anger in him right now, they'd generate one hell of a charge.

The head commander-in-chief Obama keeps demanding that Georgie tell them where the box is—the "fleshy" or "zeepy" box, if I'm hearing him correctly. Since Georgie has less of a clue than I do, the little Obama keeps tapping him with the exposed wires, hoping for a charge. And with each prod, Georgie is growing more and more pissed off. Dude already has a painful skin condition in the form of frequent and recurring malignant melanoma.

Thrusting his free hand out, the one in charge orders his sick Obama underlings to put a stop to their torture session. Such as it is.

"Moonlight...He is awake, yes?" he says in electronic monotone. "Moonlight, he is trying to tell us all something."

He steps over to me, careful not to trip over the long electrical extension cord attached to the modified Conair hair dryer. He pulls the tape off my mouth. I suck in a breath. The damp basement air tastes like worms. It's possible I've soiled myself. It's possible Georgie has too. Torture isn't pretty, even if it does come from an uncharged everyday hair dryer most teenage girls own.

I try to speak, but no words will come out.

Commander Obama moves in closer to me, leans the side of his head into me, so that I can whisper into his ear. Pressing the voice box against his neck, he says, "Speak to me, Mister Moonlight. Where is the zeepy box?"

"I. Don't. Have. It."

He stands up fast, as if once more making for Georgie and more hair dryer torture.

"Wait!" I'm trying to scream. But it comes out like a whisper.

He turns back.

"I do. I do. I do know where it is!" It hurts to speak. Feels like chunks of skin tearing off the back of my throat. But what choice do I have?

He's interested now. All three of them are interested, while they plant their gazes on me through those silly presidential masks.

"It's in my home."

"Where in home?" Commander Obama insists.

"I'll show you. But first you have to un-tape us, stop prodding Georgie with that Conair."

Commander Obama glances at the others. "Unbind them," he orders, no longer feeling the need to use the cancer voice box now that his Russian cover is blown. Then his eyes are back on me. "We will do this your way for now, yes? But if box isn't there, Mister Moonlight, we will torture you for real. We know how to torture you. We do good torture. Tricks we learn in Chechnya and Gori. Torture that is so slow and agonizing, you will dead wish inside this concrete hole."

"He *would wish he died*, you mean," chimes in the smaller Obama, the Conair still gripped in his right hand. "You learn nothing in English school."

"I learn how to say 'fuck' and 'you'!" barks Commander Obama. "Do not correct me when I speaking the English."

"I get it," I interject. "Yes, yes, yes, I very well get the point."

"See, ass pie?" Commander Obama says to the short Obama.

"Ass! Hole!" small Obama corrects again. "Word is ass! Hole! Yes?"

I'm fearing an all-out brawl, which might not be a bad thing. But I also want to get the hell out of that basement. I decide to lay on some Moonlight charm.

"Wow, you really know how to frighten somebody, Barack. Your English is excellent, and you really know what you're doing. In that whole torture-the-guy-in-possession-of-the-important-information kind of way. I'm gonna have nightmares for the rest of my life."

I sense Commander Obama actually smiling proudly under his rubber mask. "I can do well in this country of the brave Bambis and the soft belly, yes?"

"Yes, Mr. Obama," I say. "Only in America can a man like you grow up to be president."

CHAPTER 24

They un-tape us from the tables.

Having duct tape torn off your bare chest is torture enough. Big and short Obama get a kick out of the procedure, like they're giving us a waxing that glam chicks out in LA only dream about.

Then a fourth Obama appears on the scene. Or maybe this Obama has been there lurking in the shadows the entire time.

This one is shorter than the short one with the Conair. And smaller too. Slighter. The newly arrived little one applies some Betadine solution to Georgie's chest. Following that, the little Obama bandages him up. What we have here is a torturer with a conscience.

"Don't take this off until later," the little Obama whispers. "And those jerk-offs made me agree to all this."

The voice shocks me more than that dead-in-the-water Conair did Georgie. It's a female voice. It isn't like the others. Do I suspect dissension in the ranks?

I most certainly do.

They yank us off the tables, stand us up, replace the duct tape on our mouths with fresh tape, and bind our wrists together behind our backs. Then they lead us up the stairs and out a trapdoor to a four-door BMW with tinted windows.

No one says another word without the use of those voice synthesizers. That's when something dawns on me. For the most part, they've been super double-secret protective of their voices. Is it possible I know one of them? Otherwise, why hide your voice?

But I'm in no position to push the matter. Plus there's the issue of the smaller one. The one with the woman's voice. No way she's a part of the original gang of three who beat me to death just the other day. She's a newbie. Far smaller than her teammates. By all appearances, she's willing to blow her cover by whispering to us and by helping mend the small punctures Georgie received from that Conair wire.

Commander Obama and short Obama snuggle up into the front shotgun seat. Commander is pressed up tight against the door, yet somehow manages to hold a .9 mm on us over his left shoulder. The taller of the three Obamas gets behind the wheel, fires her up. The small female Obama squeezes in beside me, an identical .9 mm gripped in her left hand.

That's where they make their mistake.

Putting Georgie and me together like that. If I were doing the transporting, I would have placed someone in between Georgie and me. Or I would have at least put one of us up front in the middle, instead of that fireplug. That way they could prevent us from working together to undo the duct tape that binds our wrists.

To be truthful, it isn't all that difficult.

As the BMW moves slowly across a barren landscape of formerly suburban McHomes, I maneuver my wrists toward Georgie. Even with them being bound behind my back, I can do it without little female Obama or Commander Obama being the least bit suspicious. After all, they're wearing masks. They have limited or even zero peripheral vision.

Partially obscured vision is also a mistake.

The tall and wiry Georgie is able to maneuver his arms enough toward his left hip to get ahold of my wrists and to begin working his long fingers on my tape. He also has the benefit of long fingernails, as so many pot smokers do. The easier to roll a ducktail joint with. He works until I feel a tear in the tape, and then another, and finally one more.

I'm able to take it from there.

When my hands are free, I'm better able to attack Georgie's tape in the same manner. When he's free, we don't have to say a single word to one another to know what to do next. Georgie and I have known one another for a lot of years. We're as close as brothers.

We move at the same time.

Georgie going for Commander Obama in the seat in front of him, me springing my claws on the lady Obama beside me, snatching the .9 mm out of her hands, slamming her over the cranial cap with the barrel.

She falls into my lap as I swing the barrel around and press the pistol against the short Obama in the middle. When he pulls out his own piece, I blow his pumpkin head all over the windshield.

Georgie wrestles with Commander Obama while he shrieks like a teenage girl. I cock back the hammer on the .9 mm, press it up against his brain- and blood-spattered head.

"The piece. Give me the piece!"

But the driver swings the wheel hard to the right, making the car fishtail to the left, sending me and the woman in my lap against the door. Georgie falls back, and Commander Obama takes a shot that shatters the rear glass. With the tires squealing and the BMW still spinning circles, I know this is our only shot at getting out.

"Bail!"

Georgie opens his door, falls on out.

I open my door, and both I and the woman fall out. My entire right side screams in a pain so profound I'm forced to swallow a mouthful of spontaneously upchucked bile. I stand up as quickly as my broken body will allow, plant a bead on the Bimmer, trigger off three quick rounds that explode what's left of the rear and front glass.

But when it comes to driving, the surviving Obamas are presidential material. The damaged Bimmer burns rubber, and like *Air Force One* on takeoff, disappears into the thick black night.

CHAPTER 25

Dizziness sets in.

I want to collapse onto the pavement. But the pain won't allow it. Instead I slowly lower myself to the ground as carefully as old people having sex. I don't pass out this time, but I'm aware of that little piece of bullet lodged inside my brain, and for the briefest of moments, I feel myself drifting off to never-never land. It isn't exactly like an out-of-body experience because I'm not dying. But it's close enough, and I feel like my soul is once again trying to escape the blood, bone, sweat, and tears.

And who can blame it.

The three of us lie in the middle of an empty road.

Behind us in the distance I am able to recognize the fenced-off perimeter of the Albany International Airport. Civilization has all but abandoned this end of the mammoth facility. Or should I say eminent domain evicted the residents a long time ago, when the airport authority bought out entire neighborhoods in order to lengthen the runways. Evidently the houses were all torn down, but not all the basements were filled in. I'm guessing our Obama friends know all about these basements.

I somehow manage to grip the .9 mm in a trembling hand.

Georgie and the small female Obama on the ground are struggling to get up. So am I. But I make it to my feet first.

Georgie follows me. When the masked woman raises herself up onto her knees, I press the pistol barrel against her head. She witnessed me put a cap into her teammate's head just a minute ago. She knows now that I won't hold back from shooting just for the sake of making a new friend.

"Stay there," I order.

Then I pull off the mask.

The face that's revealed is a real beauty.

It also nearly causes me to pass out.

This time for real.

CHAPTER 26

The face belongs to a woman I've been seeing a lot of in the past few days. The nurse from the Albany Medical Center. The pretty one with the cleavage and the push-up bra who most definitely got a concussion-induced rise out of me as soon as I was revived from the beating her partners gave me in that downtown back alley.

I guess that explains how the Obamas were able to sneak into my hospital room. She no doubt arranged it.

"My head," she says, her words slurred. "You hit me over the head with that gun. You head-case son of a bitch."

"You've got no reason to complain," I say. "You tortured my friend with a Conair hair dryer. And you had a gun pointed at me first before I walloped you with it. Makes us even."

She's still on her knees, but she's trying to get up. "That hair dryer was meant to put more fright into you two idiots than actual electricity. It's UL tested and safety certified for scatterbrained teenyboppers."

"Oh, my bad. I take it all back. I definitely do owe you an apology. You were just doing your job. How's this for I'm sorry?" I raise my right leg, press my boot heel against her forehead, and shove her back down onto the street.

Georgie comes up on me from behind. He draws back his right leg like he wants to punctuate my remarks with a kick to her face.

"Not while she's down, Georgie. She's as good as dead anyway."

I keep the pistol on her. It's dark. But the halogen-lamp-lit airport casts enough luminescence for me to still make out her face.

"You really work at the hospital?"

"No."

"Then how come nobody saw through your act?" And what an act it was. I seem to recall tears streaming down her face after I was revived. Fake tears, to be more precise.

"It's not an act," she says from down on her back on the pavement. "I'm a registered nurse." Cocking her head, rolling her eyes. "OK, some of it was an act."

"You're a registered nurse who volunteered for the job at AMC just because some Albany PI with a bad brain was ambulanced there after your Obama friends tried to kill him."

"Nurses work for a lot of different hospitals, Moonlight. The hospitals don't employ us. Agencies do. I'm employed by the Ferguson Nursing Agency in Manhattan, believe it or not. The staff at the Albany Medical Center just assumed I was a fill-in for somebody for the day. They're always understaffed."

"OK then, whom do you work for when you're not nursing? Are they political, religious, or criminal? And why did they want me dead?"

"They don't want you dead."

"What is it they want, then?"

Still flat on her back, she looks up at me, her face not so pretty anymore, her long blond hair pulled back tight and hidden under the wool cap, her once-pert breasts somehow pressed flat under her black turtleneck sweater.

"Isn't it obvious, Mr. Moonlight?"

"The *what* is, I guess. Leave Peter Czech alone and hand over a box. Size, make, and shape unknown. But the *why* of any of that loses me."

She sits up and reaches over her head with both hands. I thumb back the trigger on the automatic.

"Take it easy," she says. "I'm just letting my hair down." She pulls away the rubber band, and her thick blond hair falls down against her shoulders. She reaches up into her sweater, unclasps something, works her hands busily for a few seconds, and out comes an Ace bandage, breasts popping up under her sweater like two plump magician's rabbits.

"Oh God yeah," she says. "That feels so much better." She issues me the sweetest pout you ever did see. Just like that she has her looks back, and along with them, some leverage.

As she slowly gets to her feet, her face gravitates toward my face, her lips looking all the more full, red, and luscious all the time. Her blue eyes, veiled with that blond hair, look good enough to swim in.

"Easy does it, Moon," I hear Georgie warn. "This little tart did a slam dance on your head inside a back alley."

"That wasn't me," she shoots back. "I had nothing to do with those goons. I wasn't even there."

"You're just a torture consultant," Georgie snaps.

"I wasn't torturing you," she says. "I never even had hold of the hair dryer. And even if it had worked, a shock from rubbing your feet on the carpet would've given you more of a jolt." Her blue eyes wide. "It wasn't throwing off any shock at all since I'd made sure to throw the switch on the ground fault interrupter. What you felt was the prick of the wire. That's all, big baby."

Georgie gives her a look like he's insulted. If he was going to be tortured, she should have had the common courtesy to do it right. Or else, yeah, he looks like a big baby. "So what are you trying to do?" he says after a beat. "Work up sympathy for the devil?" Crossing arms over chest. "That freakin' wire still hurt plenty."

"I'm merely telling you I don't get into that kind of torture crap, and what I did, I did because the sadistic Russian morons would kill me if I didn't at least go through the motions. Get it?"

Georgie looks at me like, *You believe her?*

She was nice to me in the hospital, so I do sort of believe her. So long as she isn't the one who fucked with that incision on my right side with a scalpel tip. And she's definitely not that man.

She moves in closer to me, her lips almost touching mine, her breasts pressed up against my chest. I feel what's become an all too common tight sensation in my midsection in the wake of my new concussions. Holy crap, if I don't almost lay one on her. If the circumstances were different, I would wrap her in my arms, haul her off into some dark corner.

But what the hell am I doing? Am I that much of a head case? Why can't I control myself when it comes to beautiful women? Dangerous women?

"Moon," Georgie repeats, his voice taking on the tone of a schoolmaster.

I'm hearing him but I'm *not* hearing him.

Her lips are touching mine now. I feel myself growing inside my pants. And then, the automatic is snatched from my hands, the barrel pointing in my face.

The tables, they have turned.

She takes a step back, the piece now gripped in her right hand.

"Little-known fact about the head trauma you suffered in that alley," she says. "Your concussion…the damage it does to the frontal lobe…it will make you so horny, so greedy for sex, you won't be able to exercise even the most basic good judgment. Remember that erection you raised for me when you were first brought back from the dead?"

I'm already fully aware of my little sexual problem.

"He's got a small fragment of .22 caliber bullet pressed up against his cerebral cortex," Georgie comments from behind me. "His judgment is already messed up. Or maybe you couldn't tell."

I feel a wave of shame wash over me. Maybe the Obamas are right. Maybe I should stay the hell away from Peter Czech. Maybe I should just stay inside the closed confines of my new bar, just like Lola wants. But it's too late for all that. They are convinced I'm hiding something inside a box somewhere. A box that was apparently delivered to me but for which I have zero recollection.

Nurse starts stepping away into the darkness, that piece aimed at my face the whole time.

"What's your name?" I insist. "At least tell us your real name."

"You think I'm that stupid, Moonlight? Come now. I wouldn't have revealed my identity at all had you not removed my mask."

I'm slowly shifting to the right, into my own patch of darkness.

"Easy, Moonlight," she warns, that now-repatriated pistol barrel following me. "I haven't quite figured out what to do with you yet."

I keep moving, while Georgie begins shifting himself in the opposite direction.

"Do. Not. Test. Me," she says, flipping back from one of us to the other. "I'm a perfect shot."

"You're not about to cap us both," I insist. "Not even Clint Eastwood is that fucking good."

"Try me, head case—" she starts to say. But that's when Georgie lunges at her legs, taking her down with a form tackle that would make Vince Lombardi proud. I surge forward, kick the pistol out of her hand.

Georgie and me: teamwork.

"You prick!" she screams at Georgie.

He rears back with his right hand, makes a fist.

"This is for your pals poking me with a Conair," he says, a split second before belting her between the eyes.

CHAPTER 27

We have the pistol back and we have the nurse, who is sufficiently passed out. The Obamas have taken a ride for now, and we have our relative health. What we don't have is transport.

"Ideas?" I query Georgie.

"Yeah, stay as far away from her as you can possibly manage."

"What she says is true. About me having uncontrollable sexual desires due to my most recent head injury."

Georgie concurs. "Back when I was working the basement of AMC," he explains, "a woman came in who was involved in a head-on car wreck. Her frontal lobe was injured when her forehead collided with the windshield, shattering it. She was hospitalized in ICU for days and eventually moved to the head trauma unit. In there she masturbated almost every minute of every day. Didn't matter if the door was open or who was walking in and out of the room or down the hall. Child, man, woman, priest, doctor. Didn't matter. She couldn't fill the day with enough orgasms. They eventually had to inject her with dopamine in order to control her."

We both stare down at the knocked-out blond beauty.

"So what we're saying," I say, "is I can now look forward not only to the occasional blackout or questionable decision, but uncontrollable sexual urges. Can my life become any more complicated?"

Nurse moans, shifts.

"I'm not sure if your being caught up in her spell is a result of your head injury or you simply being you."

We stand silent for a moment, while Nurse comes back around.

"Moon," Georgie says after a time. "Give me the gun."

"What? You don't trust me with it?" I ask.

"Trust is for assholes," he says.

I relinquish the hand cannon. No arguments. "You're no asshole, Georgie. You're my brother."

Back to where we started.

No ride, no mobile phone, no visible means of getting the hell out of that dark no-man's-land while in the process of kidnapping a beautiful blond nurse moonlighting as a thug. Doesn't matter that she's a criminal working with the same people who want to kill me, kidnapping is still a capital offense in New York. That means no calling the police. Besides, the police hate me anyway. Detective Clyne's driver—Beefy Super Cop Mike—and his middle finger are proof enough of that.

Behind us, in the far distance, a commercial jetliner taxies for takeoff. A glance over my shoulder reveals what looks like a 737. US Airways Nurse is awake now, trying to push herself back up from the pavement.

"Easy, blondie," Georgie says, holding the barrel on her.

"Don't call me that," she whispers, her voice groggy. "Now. What?"

"We haven't gotten that far yet," I say. "Got your cell phone on you?"

"You're kidding, right?"

Two headlights cut white parallel tubes out of the thick night.

"Christ," Georgie says. He drops down on one knee, the .9 mm gripped in his right hand, left hand wrapped around the shooting wrist, combat position.

I take hold of Nurse's arm, hold it tight.

"If it's the Obamas come back for the blond, I say we shoot her in the back and make a run for it."

"Agreed," Georgie says, shooting me a wink of his right eye.

"Don't I get a say in this?" she poses.

"Sure," I say. "Let's absolutely talk this thing out."

Behind us the jet screams as it lifts off from the runway.

The vehicle comes closer until it's fully visible in the road. It stops and a door opens. Georgie stands up, thumbs back the hammer on the automatic, and stuffs the barrel into the waist of his jeans. "Lola." He grins. "Freaking Lola. I don't know how it's Lola, but what a goddamned sight."

My girlfriend's standing beside her Humvee. "We don't have a lot of time," she says. "They're coming back...for her." Her eyes on our blond prisoner. "Let's move."

I don't bother to ask how she knows we're here or how she's aware of the Obama-masked thugs coming back for us or having kidnapped us in the first place. The questions can wait. I just drag Nurse over to Lola's Humvee and stuff her up into the backseat. Behind me, the sound of the airliner is fading as it climbs up into the friendly skies. Wonder if anybody in that plane has any inkling of how unfriendly things are getting down here on solid ground.

CHAPTER 28

Lola pulls a fast U-turn that takes the Hummer up onto the grassy shoulder. Crazy-illegal driving maneuvers don't matter at this point. The suburb has been bulldozed into a concrete nothing. No one will see us out here. She burns off some serious fuel motoring us down the empty street.

Georgie's taken the shotgun seat while I sit in the back with Nurse.

I see Lola's eyes framed into the rearview.

Nurse locks onto them too. "Do I tell him, or do you tell him?" she says to Lola, voice still groggy.

Georgie holds a gaze on Lola over his left shoulder.

I hold a gaze on blond Nurse over my right.

"You two know each other," I say, feeling my heart drop into my left boot.

"Surprised?" Nurse asks.

"Richard." Lola sighs. "Meet my little sister, Claudia."

Claudia holds out her hand.

I refuse it.

"I have some explaining to do?" Lola says, hooking a left away from the dark airport perimeter road and onto the main drag.

"You have to ask?" Georgie says.

My girlfriend glares at me in the rearview. I know those eyes like I do my own. But somehow, the person behind them is becoming more and more of a stranger to me by the second.

"I didn't know you had a sister," I mumble. But it's such a gross understatement, I find myself shaking my head.

"There's a lot you don't know about me, Richard," Lola admits.

"Ain't that the truth," I say.

Claudia just laughs.

CHAPTER 29

We drive into the city, and soon we're entering the state university campus. I ask Lola why she's driving us there. No one will think of looking here, she replies.

"As in those masked bastards Claudia here chose as her friends," Georgie says.

"I'm right here," Claudia responds. "You can say that shit to my face."

Georgie rears around, points a pistol barrel at her precious mug.

"And I'm right here," he barks. "We're not done talking about that little Conair electrocution game you people played with my chest."

"Get over yourself," Claudia snaps. "I did you a favor by convincing them to use the hair dryer. Left up to those meatheads, they would have cut your nuts off and fed them to you with a six-pack of Bud." She snorts. "Con-fucking-Air! Frat boys do a hell of a lot worse for initiation ceremonies. Wasn't even drawing a charge, dumb-ass big baby."

Georgie holds his ground with the pistol.

"Still felt like hell. And I don't like being scared. I was scared in Nam sometimes. I accepted that. But here, I will not accept it." He grows a smile. "Even if you do own a pair of the nicest-looking titties I've ever seen."

Lola hits the brakes.

The hummer stops on a dime.

"Let's get one thing straight," she barks. "Georgie, you're not going to shoot my sister, and you're not going to comment on the size or shape of her breasts. No matter what trouble she's got herself involved in, she's still my little sister. Got it?"

Georgie's smile fades into a pout. He retracts the pistol, turns back around. Judging by the slight trembling in both his hands, I know that he's dying for a joint. I can only hope that whatever pain he's feeling has to do with being poked with an electrical wire and not his come-and-go cancer.

"Yes, ma'am," he says under his breath. "Always got to do it a woman's way."

Lola's eyes back in the rearview. "Claudia," she says, "I don't know what you've done with these men, but Richard is my boyfriend, and Georgie is his best friend."

"I know who they are!" Rolling her eyes.

"If any further harm comes to them, you'll have to answer to me. Understood?"

"Sure thing, sis," Claudia says, acid in her voice. "But if it weren't for me, you'd be introducing them as your dead boyfriend and his even *more* dead best friend."

We drive for another half mile or so into the center of the campus, until she pulls into a faculty lot, parks in her designated space.

"My office," she orders. "And keep your heads down. You might not see them, but there're surveillance cameras all over the damn place."

"Then I'll be sure to smile," I say, "even if my heart is about to break."

CHAPTER 30

Lola unlocks the door to the lab building, and we all slip inside. The hall lights are on, but since it's so late at night, the place is empty, other than the caged monkeys. And the smell. Monkey droppings mixed with monkey piss.

For the first time since she rescued us from that empty roadside by the airport, I can see that Lola is wearing tight black jeans, a black sweater, and boots. She also has a black leather jacket on, her long hair tied back tight. Even under the circumstances...even though I'm more convinced than ever that the person I've been sleeping with for a bunch of years is not the person I thought she was...just the sight of her robs me of precious oxygen.

The four of us waste no time heading to Lola's office, Georgie behind us, the .9 mm tucked in his jacket pocket, Lola curiously not complaining about it, as if she doesn't trust her quote, "little sister," unquote, any more than we do. Between the muted screams and yelps of the monkeys, their feral smell, the bright lights, and the strange company, the moment seems at best surreal.

I remember the first time I met Lola in my backyard. She arrived unannounced on a fact-finding mission. She and my then-wife,

Lynn, belonged to the same gym, and Lola wanted to find out about some private lessons a personal trainer was conducting there. Lynn and I were not only on the skids at the time, but I had already reserved a date for a moving van to come and pick up what little stuff I could truly call my own inside our North Albany home. From there I would play the sad son-of-a-bitch prodigal son and move back into the old man's funeral home.

Up until that time, I'd spent the better part of my days chasing down bad guys as an APD cop. But I'd spent the darkest part of the nights chasing down Jack Daniels.

I stood stone stiff and looked into Lola's big brown eyes like they weren't really eyes. Like they were magnets that pulled me in. She was wearing a red bandana over her head, and her long, dark brown hair was tied into pigtails. She was dressed in farmer's overalls, and she wore black Adidas flip-flops. She was also smoking a cigarette.

She was taken aback by my gaze, which remained locked on her for more than a few seconds. Finally she smiled. "I'm Lola," she said, shooting me a quizzical look that was neither inviting nor offensive. "Is, ah, your wife at home?"

"I'm Richard," I answered. "Are you, ah, married?"

She giggled, but I think it was the result of shock, not levity.

"Lynn," I added after a beat. "She's in the back."

I opened the gate and Lola walked through, giving me a whiff of her rose petal scent. I wanted to tell her my wife and I were no longer going to be a couple in a matter of days, but I knew that would be pushing it. What I did know, however, was that as soon as it was humanly possible, I was going to find out Lola's last name and her phone number. Then I was going to call her as soon as I stepped foot inside my new home, even before I pulled the tape off the first box. My only hope was that she wasn't married.

Turns out she wasn't married.

Married anymore, that is. She'd had a brief marriage to a copywriter who was the single father of a little girl from a previous relationship. It all went bad when he started communicating with his ex-girlfriend, who was also the mother of his child.

She agreed to see me for coffee not because she liked me or even felt sorry for me. She'd known for quite a while that Lynn and I were breaking up, and she also knew what a hard bitch my head-nurse wife could be. During coffee, she even revealed that part of the reason she came to my home that evening wasn't to see Lynn at all but to get a glimpse of me. We sat across from one another at a Starbucks and her face turned as red as that bandana she'd been wearing just the other day.

We went back to my place that afternoon, and despite what the pros will tell you about first dates, we made love right there on the floor of my dad's old West Albany funeral home on top of a blanket I'd pulled out of a moving box. Later on we switched from coffee to wine, and we ate Chinese right out of the containers with chopsticks and listened to music on a portable stereo by candlelight. And then we made love again.

She revealed that she grew up in a house with a rich dad and that her parents were divorced too. That she'd had enough of marriage and if I had marriage in mind, our little relationship, as pleasant as it was, was probably going to be brief. I told her I couldn't even contemplate marriage for the moment, and with a little boy to think of—a toddler—I was a million miles away from tying the knot again.

We spent the night together on that floor, and when I woke up in the morning, Lola was gone. Like the great John Lennon once sang, "This Bird Has Flown!" No note explaining where she'd flown off to, no voice mail or text on my cell. No evidence she'd been there or that she was even real for that matter. I called maybe ten times that week, e-mailed at least as many times, and never heard another word from her. After a couple of weeks, I had accepted it as a one-night stand. Sad as it sounded.

Then one late evening the doorbell rang. I was just about ready to head to bed. It was Lola, and she was dressed in her university lab coat. Turned out, that's all she had on. We spent another night just like our first, and then in the morning, it was the same thing. She simply disappeared.

Later that month I got hit with divorce papers from my wife and a notice that she would pursue full custody of our then three-year-old boy. I also found out for the first time that she'd been sleeping with my partner at the APD, Mitch Cane, for more than a year and that my brother-in-arms was about to move into my old home.

That night I called Lola. And called, and called. But I got no response other than her answering service. I was in a hell of a way, and I needed her like no man ever needed a woman. But she never called back. In my mind, it was official: I'd been dumped by two women and stabbed in the back by a man I thought I knew better than myself.

By the time the morning came, I'd filled up an ashtray with cigarette butts and finished off an entire quart of Jack. I sat at the table in the kitchen where, as a little boy, I'd breakfasted on Cheerios and milk with my dad. I put the barrel of a .22 caliber snub-nose to my head and pulled the trigger.

CHAPTER 31

So what do you do when you discover that your lover's sister is directly involved with the men who have been trying to kill and torture you? Correction: Russian men who have actually killed you already once before and who've tortured you. Technically speaking.

You ask for an explanation, is what you do.

Which is precisely what I do as we pile into Lola's cramped, square-shaped academic office.

I stand by the closed door, my back pressed up stiff against the solid wood slab. Lola takes her chair behind her desk, as if she's about to conduct a meeting with her colleagues. Claudia sits down in the one available chair left over, and Georgie sits on the metal desk, one foot hanging off it, the other planted firmly on the carpeted floor.

Outside the door, you can still make out the squeals of the monkeys, something I never seem to notice as much when I visit Lola during the school day when the building is full of students and profs.

"Let's hear it, Lo," I say, after a strained beat. "Come to Jesus."

She exhales a long breath, places both hands over her face, and runs them slowly down her cheeks as if removing some sort of invisible mask.

"Don't say a word, Lola!" Claudia spits. "You know the deal."

Lola's head springs up. "Don't you ever try to tell me what to do," she hisses without raising her voice. "Maybe we share the same father, but my world is entirely different from yours. You don't have to play by my rules, but I sure as hell don't have to play by yours either."

"So what's going on, then, Lola?" Georgie chimes in, crossing wiry arms over his bandaged chest. His hands are trembling even more than before. I can tell he's agitated and trying to hide it. Constant pain will do that to a man. So will pride.

"Claudia is my younger half sister," Lola says. "That much you already know. I've never mentioned her, Richard, because we don't share much in common other than a biological attachment to my father."

Claudia snorts. "Got that right." She laughs.

"But family is family," Lola goes on, "and recently, our family has been experiencing some...well, let's call it difficulty."

"What kind of difficulty?" I press. "And why did you feel like you couldn't tell me about it? Me, your sig other, of all people."

"Don't tell them, Lo," Claudia insists. "Gonna bite you in the ass. You know how Dad feels about this."

You know how Dad feels about this... I take that as a less than soft warning. I also recall the speed-dial number logged into her mobile phone with the ominous tag: "My Father." Behind me, the monkeys bang on their metal cages and screech at the top of their lungs.

Lola shoots a glance at her sister, then focuses her eyes back on me. "Someone has come back into our lives unexpectedly," she explains.

"What kind of someone?" Georgie presses.

"Someone I never thought I'd ever see again for as long as I lived." Her eyes well up, her voice becomes thick. "Someone I saw only for a brief few moments a long, long time ago. Someone whom I've thought about every day of my life since our separation. But also someone I *never* wanted to see again."

I shake my head while I watch a teardrop fall down Lola's left cheek. "What are you talking about, Lo?" I say, softly.

Claudia bursts out laughing. "Your girlfriend, Lola, got herself good and knocked up. Back when she was a teenybopper."

The hairs on the back of my neck rise to attention.

Claudia sits back in her chair, long blond hair draping her smiling face.

"When I was sixteen," Lola proceeds, "I got pregnant. Abortion was not an option for me. I had the baby. But since I was a minor at the time, my father insisted I immediately put the child up for adoption upon his birth. My dad found the adoptive parents himself."

Georgie locks eyes with me. I know we're both thinking of that twisted family photo my client handed over to me.

I'm just not ready to go there yet. "But you're Lola...Ross," I say, my stomach tightening into a knot. "It is Ross, isn't it? So if it's not, then what's your real name?"

Tears falling down both her cheeks now. "Lola...Rose," she says. "Get it?"

I feel the air escape my lungs. Yeah, I get it...Ross. It looks a lot like Rose.

"And your baby's name?"

"Peter," she says. "His name is Peter Czech."

CHAPTER 32

There have been times in my life when I suspected that someone close to me was not being open about something. What comes to mind more than any other memory is when I first suspected my wife, Lynn, of cheating on me. There are the subtle hints. You've heard them all before. The coming home late after work. The strange smells on her skin and on her clothes. The distant watery stare in her eyes when she got up the courage to look me in the face. The calls and the hang-ups. The "Caller Unknown" when I checked the caller ID. The sudden end of our sex life together. The distancing, the hatred-filled stares coming at me from across the dinner table on those few nights a month we still couldn't avoid having dinner together. Or, she couldn't, anyway.

A drinking buddy of mine once said that there are two kinds of fucking that occur in a marriage. In the beginning you fuck everywhere: in the kitchen, in the bathroom, on the dining room table. But later on, when the honeymoon is long over, a different kind of fucking occurs. Whenever you pass by your wife in the hallway she cuts into you with a heart-of-ice glare and quietly barks, "Fuck! You!"

That's how it was for Lynn and me not so long ago, but not for Lola and me. Lola was distant from the start. Loving, caring, in tune with me, but still distant. Her need for space and secrecy took some serious getting used to. But after a few years of this, I knew what to expect from her and what not to expect. What I did know was this: despite her independent nature, I still would've trusted her with my life.

And now, as I stand inside her university office, I realize there is very *little* I know about the woman who, more often than not, shares my bed. I think about the woman I saw when I was dead…the woman who was so close to embracing another man it almost looked like they were about to start undressing in front of me. And I know I'm about to hear the truth, and that I need to hear it.

But I'm not sure I *want* to hear it.

Lola begins to explain about a high school boy to whom she lost her virginity. She speaks of getting pregnant and not telling the boy, not wanting to tell him, and being even more afraid of telling her father. He was the only one she could go to, though, since her mother had long ago passed away. When she finally worked up the nerve to tell him, he never yelled, and he never raised a hand to her. She would have the baby, he told her, and she would put it up for adoption. But before that, she would leave her school while the baby came to term. Then, when all was said and done, he would send her away to a boarding school. Which is precisely the way everything played out.

"Now all these years later," Lola continues, "I receive an e-mail from a man who calls himself Peter. He found my university e-mail address after having heard I was a clinical psychologist who often wrote papers on the subject of 'the only child.' " Making quotation marks with the fingers on both her hands. "More specifically, 'the adopted child as the only child.'

He sounded somewhat knowledgeable about the subject, even if only for an amateur, and we e-mailed back and forth several times. Until one day he asked me how my father was."

"You found this strange?" Me, posing the question. "A red flag maybe."

"It just didn't sound right to me. An engineer whose hobby was clinical psychology revolving around the only child, who also happens to *be* an adopted child, and who also wants to know how my father is." Pausing, collecting her thoughts while the monkeys down below bang on their cages. "It just felt strange when he wrote that to me. 'How's your father?' I felt like I was living in a fishbowl and he was looking at me. But the truth of the matter is that he had found me."

"He came to me looking for his *father*," I chime in. "He said his mother...his biological mother...was dead. Why would he say that?" I shoot a glance at Georgie. Without speaking we both know that I've been had. Czech didn't hire me to find his old man, after all. He hired me for a different reason. Something that most definitely had to do with a secret box that I either don't recall receiving or never received in the first place.

Lola spills more: "He must have said that his mother...*me*... was dead out of anger, I guess. For me giving him up, even if I was only sixteen. I don't know. Why do these people even seek out the people who rejected them in the first place?"

"Oh, come off it, Lola," Claudia chimes in. "You didn't reject Peter. Dad did. Dad made you give him up. It's what Dad wanted." Then looking at me with that pouty face. "You see, Mr. Moonlight, Dad had an agenda."

Georgie slides off the desk. "Spill, Claudia, spill."

Lola sits back in her chair. She gazes at her sister, who by now is gazing back at her.

"You gonna do it, Lo?" Claudia says. "Or shall I enlighten them?"

"Enlighten us with what?" I say.

Coming through the door, the shrill sound of screaming monkeys.

"About how Lola's son and our father are traitors and enemies of these great United States of America."

CHAPTER 33

The monkeys are really making a racket.

Louder now, and more violent than when we first entered the academic building. I picture wiry, furry bipedal primates lunging at the cages, fangs exposed, fists banging on leathery chests. They sound like they're about to escape the cages, climb the stairs, and burst through Lola's door.

Lola notices it too. She stands. "Something's not right," she says, her brown eyes peeled on her half sister.

"Dad," Claudia says. "Those stupid-ass Russians. Could be they got in through the basement windows. Or the vent system. Or maybe the maintenance crew left a door open."

"They know we're here." Then at me. "We've got to get out of here, Richard. Go. Now. Go."

"Where exactly shall we go to, Lola, except out through this door?"

She turns. There's a window behind her desk. The big double-hung window is slightly cracked open already.

"Through there." Then she says, "Kill the lights."

She pulls back the curtains, unlatches the window.

"Georgie, you first. Richard, you're next."

"You go first," I insist.

"If my father's men find you, they will kill you. But they won't do anything to us. We're protected by blood."

Protected by blood.

This I understand. I'd do anything for my boy. Take a bullet for him.

Georgie opens the window all the way, climbs out into the darkness, inches his way down to the ground. I follow, put one leg through the open window.

"You're right behind me, Lo, right?"

I purposely ignore Claudia.

"You'll feel my breath on the back of your neck," she promises.

I pull the other leg through, jump, hit the ground beside Georgie. The pain flashes through my torso. I have no choice but to swallow it.

Behind me, no Lola.

The window slams closed.

CHAPTER 34

So that's it, then.

Lola has no intention of coming with us.

Lola *or* Claudia.

Standing in the dark behind the clinical psychology lab building with Georgie, I know precisely why. If her father discovers we're all together, then he'll have no choice but to punish her. Is it possible that the punishment could be so severe that he might kill his own daughter?

Question is, why would he punish her?

For revealing that he's a traitor? An enemy of the United States of America? What precisely does that mean? What does my client, Peter, have to do with it? Other than being the biological son of Lola, the biological grandson of her dad, Harvey Rose?

One thing is for certain: I have uncovered the truth behind my client Peter Czech. He's a liar and he's playing me, Captain Head Case, for the fool. He's also Lola's biological son.

I love Lola.

I'll say it again, I love Lola Ross (or is it Rose?), and even if she is conducting an affair behind my back, I'm going to protect her and defend her. Because that's what bleeding hearts and head cases like me do. That means getting to the bottom of just what Czech and Rose are doing and how it constitutes their being traitors. It also means uncovering the importance of a certain box, and why Rose's men are willing to kill, maim, and torture for it.

I glance over my shoulder at Georgie.

"Well, old man, ready to make a run for it?"

"What the fuck," Georgie says.

"That's what I say, Georgie: what the fuck!"

Together, we run away into the black night.

Away from Monkeyland.

CHAPTER 35

We make it back to Georgie's place just before the dawn. We're safe here, or so I try to convince myself. Georgie's got no credit cards, no telephone, no forwarding address. His mother used to own the house, still owns it on paper, and she's long dead. In terms of tangible ID, Georgie might as well be just as dead. Rose doesn't know who Georgie is or where he lives. Neither does Czech or Claudia. And Lola would never divulge the old pathologist's address to her under any circumstance. At least, that's what I'm betting on, and I still have to believe it's probably a good bet.

Since both our cells are history, I call Czech via a Skype account from Georgie's computer. But all I get when his answering machine picks up is a loud humming sound. The service won't allow me to leave a message, as though it's full or not working right. I try his mobile, and I get something even more unsettling: "The caller you have reached is either disconnected or out of service."

The Peter Czech I know lives by his BlackBerry. The freedom of modern digital communications provides him a direct extension to legs that no longer work. For him not to be connected means that he's paralyzed in yet another way.

I grab two beers from Georgie's fridge and hand him one. We settle ourselves in the living room, the curtains closed, the lights off, the rising sun that filters into the room through the thin drapes casting a red-orange hue on the floor-to-ceiling stacks of vinyl record albums and posters from the 1960s, including a big poster of Richard "Tricky Dick" Nixon framed upside down.

I sit down hard on the end of the couch, pop three Advil I stole from Georgie's medicine cabinet, and wash them down with a deep drink of beer.

"OK," I say, wiping foam from my mouth with the back of my hand. "So here's the deal. My client is not who he says he is. He's not looking for his father. Nobody knows who his father is or cares to know. That leaves his mother, whom he most definitely knows and, by all indicators, loves. That mother just happens to be my current significant other."

"Don't forget Claudia," Georgie says from his perch at the window, where he's keeping a watch on the city street outside while rolling a much-needed breakfast doobie. With his now trembling hands, it isn't the easiest of operations.

"I haven't forgotten Claudia, the nurse who greeted me when I was resurrected just a few days ago. She just happens to be the younger sister of said sig other. Imagine the coincidence."

Georgie lights the joint, sucks in a big lung-inflating hit. Then he exhales. The room fills with the good smell of medicinal buds. It's as close as I come to smoking it.

"Finally," I go on, "Claudia reveals that Lola's father and her son are traitors. Traitors acting together. Whatever that means."

"Means they're selling secrets, probably to the Russians." He licks the ducktail end of the joint to seal it. "What the hell else could it mean, Moon?"

Something dawns on me then.

"Czech is an engineer at Knolls Atomic. His granddaddy Rose is your average accountant who used to work for the same feds who used to oversee the Knolls program."

"You told me Lola described him as a businessman."

I head back over to Georgie's laptop, take it with me back to the couch. Since there's no way in hell the security personnel who guard the grounds of the Knolls atomic plant are going to allow us through the gates, I decide to take the next best approach. Once again, Google.

I type in "Knolls atomic plant."

Turns out, the secure nuclear facility maintains a flashy Web site, complete with the operation's "Mission," which is none other than providing, and I quote, *"superior nuclear propulsion systems for US Naval ships by designing the world's most technologically advanced, safe, and reliable reactor plants and systems, supporting the operating fleet of nuclear ships, and training the sailors who operate them."*

The propaganda is followed up with slogans that seem lifted from right out of the old USSR Cold War Bible. Slogans like "Teamwork: We Work Better Together!" And "Loose Lips Will Sink Ships: Be a Patriot! Report All Suspicious Activities to Your Supervisor!"

The rest of the Web site is all about employment opportunities and military links. There are happy-at-work-in-the-nuke-lab photos of lab geeks, and full-color action shots of our navy's submarines diving or crashing up through the ocean's surface like big mechanical blue whales.

It's all very important looking, and it's tantalizingly apparent that the secrets harbored behind the electrified fences of the Knolls atomic power plant might indeed be of considerable value to our old Russian friends. And apparently Rose recognized that value so clearly he was blinded by the big bad bright lights and the dollar signs that would surely follow.

I kill the link, turn back to my big brother. "How much does your average accountant pencil pusher make per year, Georgie?"

He smokes a little more of his medicinal joint, cocks his head in thought. "A good accountant can pull down one hundred large per year. Even working for the feds. Especially if he moonlights during tax season."

"Good money for your basic, average, garden-variety Joe. But not for somebody with a hard-on for all the riches in the world…and willing to do anything to get it."

"Even if it means selling off your only grandchild…your daughter's only child."

"I wonder what kind of pad Rose lives in and why he's so difficult to locate on the public radar? Be interesting to find out."

"We know he can afford to hire a small army of Russian tough guys to rough people up."

"And he's willing to kill to protect what's his."

"Like that missing box for instance."

I close the laptop lid, stand up, down the rest of my beer. "We need to do some fieldwork, Georgie. We need the contents of that box or container or whatever the hell it is."

"What kind of container, Moon?"

"I'm banking that we'll know it when we see it."

He looks at me. "We get hold of it, we hold all the cards."

"We hold all the cards, we have the leverage we need to find out just what Czech and Rose are up to, how they might be traitors, and the identity of the bastards who killed me in order to keep it a secret."

"And more importantly, Moon?"

"I'm listening."

"You get to find out how deep your girlfriend is involved in all this crap, and if she really is cheating on you."

"Oh yeah." I swallow. "There's that."

CHAPTER 36

Georgie's van is still parked out front of my building down inside the abandoned Port of Albany. But we can't very well go back there. Place is way too hot. But his old orange Volkswagen Beetle still works. It's in "optimum condition," as Georgie puts it, the former-hot-wire-man-turned-pathologist having rebuilt it in his spare time over a period of twenty years.

We're driving in the orange Beetle out of the city, in the direction of Czech's suburban house on Orchard Grove. In the early morning, with the newly risen sun hidden by cold gray clouds, the streets are about as empty as Armageddon itself.

"There's just one thing that bothers me," I say, after a time. "Why would Czech hire me in the first place?"

"Because you're Lola's boyfriend?"

"But why get me involved? And why do it based upon a lie?"

"My guess is that, for whatever reason, Czech hired you to expose Rose."

"But they're partners."

"Doesn't mean they like each other very much anymore."

"You really think they're traitors, Georgie? Like the fucking Rosenbergs?"

"Yes, I do. Claudia explicitly said that both Peter and her father were traitors. You don't make that shit up." Georgie tokes on his still-lit joint, taps the fiery end on the tip of his callused tongue, and stores the roach in a pocket on his leather jacket. As he drives I notice that his hands are no longer shaking, his face no longer showing signs of pain. No tight jowls, no grimaces. "But in exposing his grandfather," he goes on, "Czech most certainly will be exposing himself."

"Doesn't make sense, does it?"

"Not yet anyway," Georgie admits. Then suddenly, "We gotta make a pit stop, Moon."

He twists the wheel, hard right, pulls off the main road and into an alley that leads to an aluminum overhead door that I recognize. It's a body shop. But not your everyday, advertise-in-the-Yellow-Pages body shop. It's an anonymous body shop with no sign mounted to the old brick wall outside to alert passersby to its existence. Not that much of anyone other than the occasional wino would be found passing by this narrow Albany alley.

Georgie gets out, leaves the Beetle running. He disappears inside the building through a sort of trick door that's been cut out of the overhead door. I wait inside the empty alley for maybe five long minutes before that trick door opens back up again and Georgie comes back out carrying a duffel bag.

He slips back behind the wheel of the Beetle, sets the bag between us, and unzips it. He pulls out an S&W .9 mm just like the piece that once served and protected me at the APD. He hands it to me along with three fresh clips. He pulls an identical one out for himself, stuffs the barrel into the waistband of his pants and the three clips into an interior pocket of his leather jacket. I store my weapon and clips exactly the same way.

Then, reaching into the bag once more, he pulls out two cell phones. The old-fashioned kind that flip open and have no real apps other than text messaging and picture-taking capabilities. He hands me one of the phones. "Number's taped to the back."

I look at it, then shove the phone into a jacket pocket separate from the clips.

Georgie reaches into the duffel bag one more time, comes back out with an honest-to-goodness stun gun.

"What's that for?"

"That's for me." He smiles.

"You get all the cool toys."

"Pays to have good friends in low places."

He picks up the now empty bag, tosses it into the backseat of the Beetle, and we're off to Czech's home sweet home.

CHAPTER 37

We make a drive-by of the Orchard Grove home before stopping.

Pays to be prudent.

It's only six forty-five in the morning. More than likely, Czech is still home, getting ready for work. It's a slightly overcast morning. Chilly. We drive past the home slow enough to notice if any lights are on, which they most definitely are not. Doesn't make sense. That is, unless the handicapped man likes to wheel himself around in the dark.

Moonlight the sharp-eyed.

We come around again, and this time I ask Georgie to stop in front. I'm listening to my built-in shit detector and it's telling me Czech isn't home. Since the blaze-orange Beetle sticks out like a blood blister on a newborn's butt cheek, I tell my big brother to pull back around to the main road where we can access a private drive that leads through a patch of woods behind the Czech backyard.

The backyard is surrounded by an old gray privacy fence, and the privacy fence is covered with overgrown pines and untended shrubs and bushes. The idea is to pull in there, then hide the Beetle behind the growth. That is, if a big blaze-orange bubble can possibly be hidden.

"What if whoever owns this here private drive calls the cops?" Georgie astutely points out. "You know, like the pesky neighborhood watch committee?"

"Risk," I answer him. "It's what you and me are all about."

"Stupidity too," Georgie says, driving back onto the main road and taking an immediate right onto the private drive, pulling off into a patch of trees directly behind Czech's house.

We both get out.

I feel the weight of the pistol and the clips. It's a good kind of weight to feel. We follow the privacy-fenced perimeter until we come to the slat fence that leads into the yard. Like most residential fences, it contains a gate that's unlocked and incapable of being locked. We enter the backyard through it.

The backyard is nothing special. Just a concrete patio, black wrought-iron furniture, and your basic gas cooker on wheels. The patio leads to a sliding glass door that's covered by a floor-to-ceiling curtain. There's a step leading up to the door. Must be Czech has no trouble negotiating the step. This isn't especially damning: the wheelchair-bound can learn to negotiate some pretty formidable obstacles.

Georgie and I look at one another and approach the slider. He already has his Swiss Army knife out and ready to jimmy the lock. But the closer we come to the door we can see that jimmying won't be necessary. There's a fist-sized hole in the glass, and a long, spider-veined series of cracks in the rest of the glass. Obviously we aren't the first ones to visit the Czech household this morning.

"Fix bayonets," Georgie says, sounding a lot like his old Vietnam grunt self.

I draw the .9 mm, slide back the bolt, and allow a round to enter the chamber. I thumb the safety off.

Georgie does the same.

When I give him the nod, he sticks his right hand carefully through the existing hole, grabs hold of the opener, and slowly slides the door open. Pulling back the curtain, he takes a step inside, and like Alice, disappears through the sliding glass.

CHAPTER 38

I follow close behind the old platoon leader while he takes point.

The place is dark and smells like must and sweat. There's the faint scent of some bacon having been cooked recently. Probably isn't all that easy for Czech to clean the joint. Not on a daily basis.

Georgie stops, runs his hand along the wall in search of a light switch. When he locates it, he flicks it on. Forget clean. The place has been left in a shambles. It's been flipped, no doubt about it. Ransacked. Couch overturned, chairs tossed onto their sides, green Astroturf carpeting torn up with a blade so that whoever did this could get a look at what might be hidden underneath it.

It's the same story in the kitchen, dining, and living rooms.

Glass shattered everywhere. Drawers and cabinets opened, bookcases pulled away from the walls, the books torn open and shredded, carpeting ripped up, holes punched through the Sheetrock walls.

When we check the garage, the car is gone. And when we check the basement, the space is empty, other than about two dozen empty boxes piled up in the middle of the floor, the name Ashline Movers printed on the red tape that's secured them.

There's a set of snow tires piled up in one corner and some old furnace filters leaning against the boiler. Otherwise nothing.

Our .9 mms at the ready, Georgie and I head back upstairs and check the bathrooms. The medicine cabinets have been tossed. No surprise there. Broken mirror and glass cover the sinks and toilets, the overhead light reflecting off the shards like mini fun-house mirrors. All manner and type of pill bottles lie on top of the shards of glass. Staring down at the mess, I can't imagine a big box being hidden inside something as narrow as a medicine cabinet. But then, what the hell do I know? I'm just the jerk who's given his life once already for this project.

After we're through with the bathrooms, we have one last room to check out. It's located immediately off the front vestibule: Czech's combination bedroom/office.

The bed sheets have been ripped away, the mattress ripped open in several places with a blade. Same for the box spring, which has been removed and is now leaning up on its side against a far wall. A nightstand has been tipped onto its side next to the smashed clock radio it used to support, and the dresser drawers have all been pulled out, their contents—clothes, underwear, handkerchiefs, jewelry, Depend undergarments, and who the hell knows what else—tossed on the floor into a pile. Even Czech's shoes—all either loafers or specially made adult Velcro models—have been examined.

What the hell kind of box are the Obamas looking for?

Of course, the desk hasn't been spared a good ransacking. The drawers have been opened, their contents dumped out. Same with the rolling drawers on a giant metal filing cabinet, their files and their contents spilled everywhere. Some black-and-white banker's boxes, like the kind my dad used to store the funeral parlor's tax records in, have been yanked from the closet and dumped.

I have to wonder about the banker's boxes.

Is a banker's box the kind of box the Obamas have been talking about?

"Think they found what they were looking for, Moon?" Georgie poses.

"The mysterious zeepy or flesh box," I say, a little under my breath. "I'm listening to my built-in shit detector, Georgie, and I'm voting *no*. No way the flip would have been this thorough otherwise."

But something else is wrong with this scene, and if I know Georgie as well as I think I do, I know he can sense it too. Together we look into one another's eyes and swim in the weighted silence.

Until Georgie breaks it by telling me he has a quick story he wants to share.

"There was this guy," he begins, "went to his doctor complaining of migraine headaches. Said he got them every day. He couldn't work, couldn't function, couldn't eat or drink. Guy's life was just a total wreck. So the doc examines him, determines he's got a rare disease. His testicles are positioned too close to his spine. They're pressing up against his nerves, causing the headaches. The only cure, of course, would be total testicular extraction. Guy with the headaches was in such pain, he agreed to emergency surgery.

"He wakes up from the operation and never before has he felt so good. So good, in fact, he wants to treat himself to a custom-tailored suit upon his hospital release. So he heads to an expensive Jewish tailor. Jewish tailor gives him one looks and says 44 long. The guy is amazed at how knowledgeable the old tailor is. Tailor looks him over further, says 38/14 for the shirt and 34/34 for the trousers. The guy is just positively floored at how much this old dude knows. But then the tailor says, for underwear, 36 or 38. The guy says, 'No way, sir, I'm a 34.' 'No, no,' insists the tailor, 'on you, 34s would be so tight they'd press your balls up against your spine.'"

Georgie laughs. But there's a lesson to be learned here, no doubt. Just because something appears to be broken doesn't mean it's actually broken.

"Take a look here, Moon," he says, reaching into the top drawer on the file cabinet. "I'm nearly six feet and I have trouble reaching all the way into the back of this thing. How the hell was Czech going to do it from a wheelchair?"

"Plus those banker's boxes up on the top shelf of the closet. He couldn't exactly have climbed a stepladder."

"The dishes in the kitchen cabinets, the books on the bookshelf, the pills in the medicine cabinet...all unreachable for a guy who's in essence not even three feet tall."

We head back into the kitchen, take one more look around. In the adjoining vestibule is a closet that we haven't opened yet. I go to it, open the door.

"Czech is more than just a traitor," I say.

"Explain," Georgie pushes.

"I think he's perfectly capable of walking," I say, staring down at his unoccupied wheelchair.

CHAPTER 39

There are explanations, of course, for how a disabled man can have boxes stored on the top shelf of his closet and files of papers in the top drawer of his filing cabinet. There are logical reasons why he'd have meds, plates, and drinking glasses stored in areas he can't reach, just as there are valid explanations why he might have boxes stored in an otherwise empty basement. The most obvious explanation is that Czech has someone help him from time to time. Perhaps even regular help on a daily basis. Many handicapped persons, no matter how independent, depend upon the assistance of others just to get through a single routine day.

Which is exactly how I explain it to Georgie while getting back inside his Beetle. And Georgie, being a medical man by trade, couldn't agree more.

He turns the engine over, throws the manual tranny into first.

"But how do you explain the wheelchair?" he poses.

"If he's lying about who he is," I answer, "then I guess he doesn't need it. At least, he doesn't need it in private. Or maybe he's got more than one chair. Or it's possible he was kidnapped without it by the same people who roughed up his house. The Russian Obamas, no doubt, upon orders from Grandpa Rose."

"Which leaves us where?"

I never get a chance to answer before the bullet pierces the rear and front windshields.

CHAPTER 40

Georgie slams his right foot flat on the gas, the tires spitting dirt and gravel. "Kiss the rubber mats, Moon!"

I drop down as far into the well as I can, the cold gunmetal on the .9 mm pressed against my right cheek. I'm not a big guy. But I'm not Yoda either, and I immediately begin to cramp up in the tight space.

They—the Russians—must have been watching us scope out Czech's crib, hoping that we'd uncover what they apparently could not: a box filled with something important.

Georgie's speeding down the private drive unaware of what awaits him at the end. That much I know for sure. I poke my head up enough to get a shot off and at the same time make out a big black GMC with tinted windows, a single hand exposed out the passenger-side window, a good old-fashioned silenced Uzi attached to the hand.

The Uzi spits fire and a couple of rounds take out the back windshield. I drop myself flat onto Georgie's lap.

"Faster!" Me shouting.

"Fuck do you want me to go?"

He starts spinning circles on the lawn at the end of the drive.

Another burst of fire and the driver's-side window explodes.

"Twenty years of tender loving care!" Georgie shouts. "Not another Beetle like this in the world except for on the *Abbey Road* album cover!"

He pushes me off.

"Fuck are you doing?"

Another burst of rounds sink into the flat, metal VW dash.

"Enough!" Georgie barks. Crazy old bastard stops the Beetle in the middle of the lawn, that big black soccer-mom GMC bearing down on us like one of Rommel's Tiger Tanks. Georgie pulls back on the emergency brake, opens the door, gets out. What he does next is nothing short of miraculous and suicidal.

With only the open door to protect him, he stands his ground.

"Fuck with me, but not my ride!" he shouts, rounds pinging against the door and churning up grass and dirt.

He then proceeds to raise his Smith & Wesson slowly, calmly, left hand clutching his right wrist, combat position. Finger pressed against the trigger, he empties the entire clip into the GMC, stopping it dead in its tracks.

When it's over, a heavy quiet fills the air.

Off in the distance, the sound of cruiser sirens can be heard. I know the sound well. I was a cop once. A good one. Before my head got scrambled. We have to haul ass out of here. Do it now.

I crawl out of the Beetle, stand up. Maybe too fast. My head starts spinning. I've experienced that same sensation before. The world spinning at my feet, the feel of my body lifting off the ground. The feeling of utter weightlessness. Not exactly my soul leaving my body again—more like I'm about to lose consciousness. My brain, it isn't right. Under stress, the blood speeding through the veins and capillaries swells my brain around that piece of .22 caliber bullet.

Moonlight tilts.

I raise my automatic to try to give Georgie some backup as he approaches the now quiet GMC on foot.

It's the last thing I remember before passing out.

CHAPTER 41

In the dream you're dead.

Big surprise there.

You're floating over a mechanical bed inside a private hospital room. The room is white and brightly lit with angelic rays and bursts of brilliant sunlight. Your body is laid out on its back in the bed. You have this smile planted on your face like you're happy to finally get the hell out.

Standing by your side is Lola. She's dressed in a long white gown, her long, lush dark hair draping her face like a black veil. Covering her eyes are those round Jackie O sunglasses. Tears are streaming down her face, and she's holding tightly to your hand.

When the door opens, a second person enters the room. It's Some Young Guy. He's faceless again, his face not really a face, but an oval-shaped blur or a mask. He stands on the opposite side of you, looking down upon your prone, motionless body. He then reaches out his right hand over you as if offering it to Lola. She drops your hand and takes his. That's when Some Young Guy reaches into his pants pocket with his free hand, pulls out a big white diamond engagement ring. He slips the ring onto Lola's finger.

"Will you marry me?"

"I will," she answers, her face lit up like a glowing moonbeam. "I will. I will. I will."

Together they consummate their new vow with a long, slow kiss, directly over your shattered corpse.

When I come to, there's a man lying on the grass beside me. Guy's kicking up a storm and trying to scream, but Georgie's stuffed a rag in his mouth. The rag he uses to check the Beetle's oil level.

Subdued Guy is dressed in black and his ankles and wrists are bound behind his back with the same plastic portable Hefty Bag cuffs that I used to apply to drunk and disorderly perps back when I was still a cop. The guy is about average height but big. Stocky. Maybe five-nine or ten. Two hundred twenty pounds if I have to guess. Big enough that I can't imagine how all one hundred sixty pounds of skin and bones Georgie managed to subdue him. But when I see the old pathologist kneel down and zap the man with the stun gun, I'm no longer kept in the dark.

Georgie spots me. "Moon! You blacked out."

Oh yeah, I blacked out.

Cop sirens off in the distance. Getting louder by the half second.

A big guy lying beside me.

Stun guns and real guns.

Oh yeah, a shootout. I was in a shootout. Just a minute ago. Behind a house. Peter Czech's house. Shootout, behind the house. A black GMC with tinted windows. Russians. Russians who want something. A box.

Sirens.

The cops getting closer. Lying there on the grass, I estimate their ETA to be no more than a few minutes. It tells me I've been passed out for only a few seconds at most.

"Can you get up, Moon?"

I lift myself up, feeling that familiar resettling sensation that my brain always experiences after an episode. Kind of like the weights drawing back on a doll's eyes when you stand her upright, while your brain reboots all of its memory programs. Let me try and remember, did I save my settings before logging off? Or did my brain save my settings for me?

"What are we gonna do with him?" I pose in a groggy voice.

"He's our leverage and our navigator," Georgie answers. "Help me stuff the son of a bitch into the back of the Beetle."

"We can't just take the GMC?"

Georgie shoots me a look.

"There's a dead driver in there and blood and brain matter, and the freaking police are on their way. Any more questions?"

I know better than to argue with my big brother, even if this is my show.

Me being the physically bigger man, I grab hold of the goon's shoulders, while Georgie grabs hold of his legs. Dropping him onto the backseat, we push and shove his stocky body into the cramped space with all the grace and finesse of a pair of slaughterhouse butchers. It's like packing two pounds of shit into a one-pound barrel, and both Georgie and I scrape the backs of our hands and bruise the tops of our skulls getting it done.

Before we bolt the scene, Georgie grabs the thug's Uzi, aims it directly at the windshield of the GMC, and fingers off the remainder of the clip. The entire glass plate explodes, along with what's left of the driver's head. He then wipes the weapon of prints and brings it back with him to the Beetle. Lifting up the still catatonic goon's hand, Georgie presses the guy's fingers and palm against the weapon, making sure to leave some noticeable print impressions. Then the old pathologist tosses the still smoking weapon to the ground.

Hopping back behind the wheel, Georgie revs the engine.

I barely make it into the passenger seat before the tires resume spitting grass and gravel.

CHAPTER 42

Georgie doesn't opt for the easy, take-the-long-way-home kind of smooth mobile escape. Instead he motors the Beetle through a small patch of woods located on the opposite side of the private drive. The car rocks and rolls and scrapes and pounds its way through the thick brush until we come to the other side, which turns out to be some poor suburbanite's backyard.

Georgie never pauses to contemplate going around the yard. Instead he throws the tranny into fourth gear and motors right on past the swing set and the clothesline.

Who the hell still uses a fucking clothesline?

He makes for the front yard, speeding across the manicured lawn and then jumping the curb back onto the quiet suburban street.

My head is still reeling.

I'm not feeling dizzy anymore. I know the danger of passing out again is all but gone. But I also recognize something else happening inside me. It isn't a physical sensation so much as a transformation. A temporary loss of bearing. Like a captain piloting a rudderless boat in thick fog.

What's just happened?

A gunfight...roger that...check.

Outside Peter Czech's house...check.

Dead people inside a black GMC...dead Russians...check.

Russians want a box...check.

Cops chasing us...check and double check.

I look down at my lap. I'm gripping the .9 mm. I have no idea how the gun got there. I only know that it's mine, and that it's a good thing that I'm still holding it.

We head north on Route 9 toward the city, Georgie taking it easy, to not attract unwanted attention.

No more sirens.

No sign of the police behind us, beside us, or ahead of us.

Check and triple check.

"Georgie," I say, after a time, "who exactly is the dude in the backseat again?"

"Oh shit," he says. "Short-term memory kicking out on you."

Short-term memory. Let's review today's headlines, shall we?

Russians want a box...roger that and check.

Gunfight in back of a house...check.

Whose house?

Shit, whose house?

Wheelchair, BlackBerry in hand, thin mustache, one pint Jack and Coke...

Peter Czech. Czech's house...check.

Gun in my hand. Oh, yeah. Gunfight. Check.

OK, Moonlight, get your shit together.

I'm not sure how to put this delicately, but beneath my gun, my lap has grown stiff and full. I'm sporting a road boner...and damn if it isn't in some painful need of relief.

Concussions...check.

Multiple concussions...check.

Concussions on top of a bullet frag lodged in brain...check.

Declared dead just days ago...check.

Brought back to life. Double and triple check.

"Take a breath," Georgie insists. "It's the concussion. Your memory will come back to you. Trust me."

My memory. It always comes back to me. So do these boners.

Behind us, the guy jammed down into the backseat squirms like a gut-shot rabbit. He starts kicking the seat and screaming into his oil-rag gag.

The Jimmy Dean in my pants is getting huge. Too big for the Beetle.

But that doesn't stop the need for immediate relief.

"Listen," I say, "you gotta stop off at the gas station or something. I mean it."

I nod down at my lap, lifting the cold hard steel of the .9 mm just enough to reveal the hot hard flesh that's pushing up my pants. Meanwhile, the guy in back is pounding on the Beetle wall and kicking the crap out of our seatbacks. Reaching into his leather jacket, Georgie pulls out the stun gun. While keeping his eyes on the road, he thrusts the business end of the stun gun against the big man's ribs. The electrical jolt puts him back out.

Now it's me who's squirming, feeling like I'm about to explode.

"What you're experiencing," Georgie, the retired pathologist, explains, "in your head. In your pants. It's temporary." He can't resist a giggle.

Cops are likely on our ass, and I, a forty-eight-year-old man, am sporting a raging road boner, like a kid on the school bus.

"Pull over, Georgie. I'm fucking telling you, dude."

He yanks into a Mobile gas station, pulls around back near the Dumpster to hide the Beetle. "Go do what you gotta do," he says. "Just make it quicker than quick."

"Maybe they'll let me borrow a *Playboy* off the rack," I say, opening the door.

"*Penthouse* is better. Go!"

I get out of the car, head for the inside of the station and the privacy of the bathroom.

How do you spell relief?

Just ask Richard "Dick" Moonlight, Captain Head Case.

CHAPTER 43

When I reemerge from the gas station bathroom, Georgie has the radio on. I get in, sit down, pull the seatbelt around me, buckle it. The news report on the radio speaks of a shootout inside a suburban neighborhood. A man was discovered dead inside a GMC, the result of severe gunshot wounds. That's when it all starts coming back to me in a less fuzzy, less punch-drunk way. The bits and fragments of short-term memory start making some sense.

"Four Orchard Grove," I recall. "Peter Czech's house."

Georgie smiles. "That's the great thing about the left brain," he offers up. "It wants to remember things the way they happened. It's the right brain that messes everything up."

As the fog lifts in my brain, I picture Lola.

"Lola," I say. "Christ, we left her and Claudia behind in Lola's office, those Obamas banging on the door. You think her old man will protect her, Georgie? Protect her from harm, those Russians get desperate enough?"

"Call her," Georgie says. "Call her now."

I pull out the cell phone, dial the number for her North Albany terrace apartment. No answer. I call her school line. I get her answering service. I hang up, call the secretary in the psychology department. She tells me Dr. Ross has yet to report to school. I ask her what time it is, like I can't just find out by looking at my watch. She says it's eight thirty-five in the morning. She also says that usually Dr. Ross would be on site by now, in her office working. Perhaps she had a doctor's appointment, she adds hopefully. Maybe a hair appointment. But I know better inside my gut.

My newly rebooted built-in shit detector is hounding me.

The goon in the backseat is still out. He's moaning up a painful storm, however.

"How fast can you make it to Lola's?" I beg of Georgie. "I'm thinking that's where the Obamas will go next now that they dug up a whole lot of nothing at Czech's house."

"I'm on it," he answers.

"Make like lightning," I say.

We speed off in the old Beetle.

CHAPTER 44

Lola lives in an apartment in North Albany that belongs to a much larger complex called Dutch Village. A series of three- and four-storied Dutch revival brick buildings constructed during World War II that look more like the dormitories for an Ivy League university than an apartment complex. I have a key to her place on my small key ring. I let us in the front door to the building, head down the steps to her bottom-floor terrace apartment.

Her door is wide open.

Like my built-in shit detector has already warned, the place is trashed, no stone left unturned; no decoration, furniture piece, or eating implement not shattered or broken. As if a smashed antique ladder-back chair was going to suddenly reveal the contents of some secret box.

Fucking Russians.

Automatics out and poised for battle, Georgie and I already know that danger no longer lurks in the five-room apartment. That the danger has come, trashed the joint, and fled.

Empty-handed. Except for Lola, and maybe her sister.

I know that if Rose is desperate enough to kidnap his own daughter, the mother of the son he sold off for profit, then she might be as good as dead.

"You feel the need to search the place?" Georgie asks.

I lower my weapon, thumb scratching the safety. "Negative." I head out the door. "I say let's just cut to the chase."

We rush back out to the Beetle. I open the driver's-side door, push the pistol barrel up against the Russian's temple. He starts to heave and kick. Georgie goes for his stun gun.

"No!" I shout.

I cock back the pistol hammer, just so the goon can hear how close he is to blood and pain and panic. Then I reach down with my free hand, tear the duct tape off his mouth.

He spits foamy saliva and mucous.

I slap him with the barrel. On the ear, where it hurts the most.

"Mother...*fucker!*" he barks. Russian accent.

I slap him again because I can.

"Keep moving like that, Boris, and I'll shoot you. Call me names again, and I'll shoot you. If you don't tell me where Rose is keeping Lola Ross, I will shoot you. Do we have an understanding, Boris?"

"Go to devil, little man!" He's grinding his teeth, feet kicking at the interior sidewall, making the whole ride rock 'n' roll.

"It's *go to hell*, Boris. That could be your name right? Boris? It's a possibility with you being Russian and all?"

I press the bad-ass end of the pistol barrel tight against his left knee.

"Boris, I need you to hold still for just one moment."

He obeys.

I pop one off.

An explosion. Instantly followed by bone and blood spatter and one former Soviet kneecap that's all but evaporated. All except a little piece of pink tendon that's hanging outside skin and torn trousers.

The goon doesn't scream. He just makes a yelp like a dog and then he starts sobbing. I didn't think Russian goons cried.

"Lola Ross. Her location. Rose must have her. Tell me now, or head back to the motherland in a wheelchair just like Peter Czech's."

"Rose, he is dead!" he cries.

"I think he's very much alive, Boris."

I aim for the other knee, pull back on the hammer. He keeps on sobbing.

"Yes, yes. Rose, he is alive. But he does not *existing* anymore."

I go back to the new wound, push the black barrel against it. He yelps, begs for me to stop. I pull back.

"Tell me he's not really dead. Tell me, Boris. Tell me he's not dead and that he's holding Lola and that you know where he's holding her."

"Nyet! Not existing. Not really dead, yes?"

"Which is it, Boris?"

"Rose's heart. It beats. His eyes. They see. His lungs. They breathe the air. But, officially, he is very, very, very fucking dead."

Click. The lightbulb flashes on bright over my head. I finally fucking get it. That explains the county record. It lists one Harvey Rose as dead. How he pulled that one off, I'll never know. But then money talks. Russian money. Mob money. Or maybe Russian government money. Putin money.

"Where does the dead Rose live?"

More crying, more yelping.

I tap the wound with the barrel.

He screams.

Outside the car Georgie stands his ground, surveying the surrounding parking lot for cops or interested bystanders. I'm assuming we're in the clear thus far. This won't take much longer, in any case. No matter which way things turn out for this Russian goon.

"Mister Rose...he lives in the Montgomery Ward building, yes? Down in the North Albany. How you call it? *Men-Yands-Land*."

"That old abandoned white elephant at the bottom of the North Albany hill," I say. "It's Menands...the Village of Menands, founded by Louis Menands. Greedy motherfucker born in Paris and immigrated to Albany in search of freedom, the American dream, and cold hard cash. You got that, Boris? He didn't immigrate to Russia for cold hard cash. He came *here* to the good old U-S-of-fuckin'-A, just like you and your greedy mobster goon friends did. And nobody lives in the Montgomery Ward building. It's a rat-infested ruin. Been abandoned for years, bro."

"That's because it is locked up tighter than gulag. Believe it. He lives there, yes? Up in white tower."

"The tower. And that's where we'll find Lola?"

"Da."

"She's alive?"

"She's his fucking daughter, man. Mister Rose, he does not kill his fucking own daughter."

I make like I'm about to pistol-whip the knee wound again.

"She is alive, alive, alive! Rose, he thinks she could be person hiding something, and he, poppa...he wants it back, yes?"

"The box. Rose wants the box."

He looks up at me, eyes slanty, forehead scrunched and furrowed in pain.

"What...fucking...box?"

Aiming for the second knee.

"I am serious man here, dude. I am on soil that is foreign, dude. What...fucking...box is it you speak of?"

"The box you guys are convinced Peter Czech handed over to me while I was still in the hospital. The one you and those other Russian porno-meat, Obama-mask-wearing monsters killed me for."

"Not one ever mention *box* to me."

"So I'm hearing things, Boris?"

That's when the injured, crying thug does something completely out of character for some poor bastard with his right knee freshly shot off. He begins to laugh. Despite the pain and the blood. Despite the fact that if and when he ever walks a straight line again he will display a permanent limp.

"Not box!" he spits, choking on his laughs, even though what's left of his knee is hanging down on his shin. "Not box, not box. But *flash* box. What you call a flash drive or *zeeepy-zip-zip* drive."

I pull the gun away.

I'll be dipped.

I heard wrong. Those synthesizers the Russian Obamas pressed up against their throats distorted the words they pronounced. No wonder I have no recollection of a box or a shoebox or a big cardboard kind of box. What they're after are computer files, and no doubt they must have been stored on some flash drive or old-fashioned zip drive that has to belong to Peter Czech.

Makes sense.

A flash drive doesn't resemble a real box. But I guess it can be confused for a little, rectangular boxlike device by a foreigner who has no idea how to properly communicate it in English. These Russian goons were literally lost in translation when they were torturing me for a fleshy or zeepy box.

"Tape him up again, Georgie," I say.

My big brother immediately goes to work on it.

I hop in the shotgun seat, pistol still aimed at the goon, while Georgie finishes wrapping him up. When he's done, I say, "Montgomery Ward building, Georgie. Boris is going to lead us directly to Harvey Rose. The dead one who's alive and holding my girl."

"It's full light still," he points out.

"Head to Moonlight's first," I agree. "Drive around back and pull up beside the Dumpster. We'll hole up there until nightfall."

"It's almost ten in the morning," Georgie points out. "I could use a cold one right about now."

CHAPTER 45

I close up Moonlight's as soon as we get inside, lock the doors after sending my senior-in-college bartender home with a full day's pay stuffed inside his jeans pocket. No one's busying himself with drinking his way through a fine fall morning other than Uncle Leo anyway. For his troubles, I send the Korean War vet home with a large to-go cup full of rum and coke.

Free of charge.

Georgie and I take turns looking in on Boris, who by now is passing in and out of consciousness. Georgie's worried that he'll bleed out all over the rehabbed Beetle before he can become of use, so he decides to suture him up as best he can, using the small sewing needle and biodegradable thread from the first aid kit mounted to the bar back. He also gives the goon a bottle of water.

Sitting back down at the same table where I first sat down with a wheelchair-bound Peter Czech, I crack open a beer apiece for us, while Georgie pulls the much-needed half-smoked medicinal joint from the pocket on his leather and fires it up.

Breathing in the pot, he sits back, exhales, much like a cigar-smoking, brandy-sniffing aficionado would do. I drink some beer. It tastes good and it's calming me down. But I know I have to limit myself to only one or two. Reflexes ain't what they used to be. And I'm finding it harder and harder these days to stay alive. But then I'm finding it just as hard to die too.

"So what's the bottom line on this train wreck, Georgie?" I pose after a beat. "In your humble pathological opinion."

"Bottom-line, no-bullshit opinion?" he says, stealing a quick sip of beer. "Rose is a spy, and probably has been one since the Cold War."

"How do you know?"

"Makes sense to me. He's old enough to be a Cold War spy, and from what you told me inside your loft, he was working as an accountant for the government on the Knolls atomic plant account. Greedy prick probably started selling secrets to the Russians from day one. Back then it was real easy to be a spy. All you had to do was set up a PO box at the direction of some Russian agent living and thriving in a local suburb, and you were in business."

"And how would you know that shit?"

"Don't you watch the History Channel, Moon?"

"Don't even have a TV, bro."

"OK, whatever. Anyway, Rose the spy likes his work and the easy cash it brings him, so he starts building an empire of his own."

"But when his daughter gets knocked up, Granddaddy Rose gets very pissed off, doesn't he?"

"Precisely, Moon. So he arranges to hand little baby Peter over for adoption. Bit of a control freak, he picks the adoptive parents himself—a Russian immigrant couple he's come across in his spy dealings and who also happen to work for Knolls. But also being a vain asshole, he makes sure he gets included in a photo of himself and the happy couple with their new baby while his daughter is off in the bathroom. No fan of loose ends, handpicking the parents is his way of keeping tabs on little baby Peter. This attention to detail pays off when Peter the adolescent happens to show an aptitude for engineering. Ends up going to engineering school and, lo and fucking behold, becoming an employee of the Knolls atomic plant. Now how's that for the warm and cozy American fucking dream?"

My big brother smiles, drinks some more beer.

"Listen, Moon. Rose must have been selling secrets for decades," he goes on. "As a fed accountant he would have audited the Knolls Atomic books. Dude must know precisely what a nuke reactor costs, where to get one, and exactly what stores sell them. And it ain't Amazon-dot-com or Lowes.

"So what a huge fucking break to have a talented, Russian-sympathizing engineer of a grandson pop up to steer toward the nuke plant where it so happens the boy's adoptive father works, and which his secret grandfather has been monitoring for ages on behalf of the feds. It's of course a risk all the way around. But what does Rose have to lose? Not a thing. He's already got a foothold in the Russian spy business. He's looking for longevity, a continuation program to keep the family business growing and thriving.

"It might have been a no-brainer for Czech. That is, so long as old man Rose was paying him and his foster parents the whole time. Or maybe Czech had no choice but to toe the red line, or face something dreadful. Like his own death or the death of his adoptive parents."

"Czech told me his biological mother died of cancer," I interject. "But he also told me both his foster parents died in an automobile accident."

"Look into it further," insists Georgie, "and I can bet that car wreck was more than just an accident. Could be that Czech wanted out. Especially after his own accident and resulting paralysis. But Rose wouldn't let him get out. And he proved how serious he was by killing the foster mother and father, made it look like an accident."

We both chew on that one for a while.

"So why now?" I chime in after a beat. "Why does Czech come to me with some crazy story about finding his father, who's really his grandfather?"

"Like I said, he wants to expose Rose for who he is."

"But in doing so he'll expose himself."

"Risk he's willing to take."

"Why?"

Georgie, shrugging narrow shoulders: "Maybe he wants to protect Lola, his mother. Maybe he wants something else from Rose and he's willing to expose him in order to get at it."

We both look at one another. Despite some pretty good guesses about what the fuck is going on in Albany, we're empty of real answers. But...

"We just might find out in a few hours just what Czech wants from his partner and grandfather," I suggest.

"I suspect we will, Moon. And let's hope that Lola is no worse for wear for her son's double-dealing."

"A mother's love for her son. It supersedes everything. Even federal and state law."

"And good old common sense."

My stomach drops at the thought of Lola being harmed and also at the thought of her having a son and a father like Rose and never revealing it to me. Then there's the question of her being disloyal to me. It's all too much to handle in one sitting. I drink down my beer, grab another from the cooler behind the bar.

Stamping out his joint and pocketing the roach, Georgie drinks down the rest of his beer, sets the empty on the table. He stands.

"Gonna check on our injured Boris," he informs. "He is a guest in our country, after all."

"Sorry about the blood all over your Beetle."

"Don't worry. Got friends who can clean that stuff up." He smiles. "Gonna cost you though."

"Put it on my tab," I insist.

"Getting to be a huge tab," he says, walking out the back door.

CHAPTER 46

I recall the old Montgomery Ward building with some affection. I remember as a kid anxiously awaiting the arrival of the Montgomery Ward catalog to my dad's funeral home. It was so big and thick, about the only books in the home that held more weight were the Bible and the phone book. For the entire fall season right up until Christmas I'd stare at full-color glossy pics of the toys I expected Santa to deliver. Train sets, electric car racetracks, cowboy six-guns, basketballs, baseballs, footballs, fishing poles. You name it, Montgomery Ward had it.

While the toys miraculously appeared for me under the Christmas tree on the morning of December 25th, every now and then the old man would splurge and allow me to pick something out from the catalog during the year. That's when we'd make the short drive to the Montgomery Ward building, which was located on lower Broadway in what then was the thriving North Albany Village of Menands. That is, before the shopping malls took over and the big stand-alone department store went belly-up and half of Louis Menands's village got laid off.

Now, instead of driving up to that wondrous, red-white-and-blue-lit, white ten-story concrete and plaster-sided building with attached warehouse, Georgie and I approach a gated and boarded-up haunted castle, long abandoned and all but forgotten. Now instead of happy shoppers coming to and fro from the parking garage next door to the old building, feral dogs and cats patrol the grounds in search of their next meal while rats scamper across the old parking spaces and crow's nest in the eaves.

If the razor-wire-topped chain-link perimeter fence screaming KEEP OUT doesn't make you want to stay away from the building, the ever-present threat of a psycho crack addict who won't hesitate to cut your belly open with a straight razor for an hour's worth of high will.

According to Boris, this is the place the officially dead but unofficially alive Harvey Rose calls home sweet home. Also the place where I hope to find Lola and Peter Czech alive.

God willing.

Since the parking garage isn't fenced off, Georgie pulls onto the first-level ramp, drives slowly up, and parks in a spot that sends some crows flying off into the black night and rats scampering for cover. He kills the lights. Reaching over me to the glove box, he opens it, pulls out a small black Maglite.

He flicks it on, shines it on the goon's knee. The one that's no longer there.

"One of us has to be Boris's legs," he points out.

It's Georgie's way of saying, *You're it!*

We both get out, face the razor-wire-topped perimeter fence.

"Wonder if it's electrified," I pose.

"Count on it. Only way we're getting in is him."

We begin the inevitable: dragging the bleeding Boris out of the Beetle. It's about as much fun as Georgie and I used to have pulling a crushed corpse from out of a car wreck prior to Dad hauling it away for autopsy and embalming, but we get him out and wobbling on his one good leg. While I act as his human crutch, Georgie keeps a close eye on his back with both the Maglite and his .9 mm.

"Let's have it, Boris," I say. "How do you normally gain access to a dead man's castle?"

I'm fully prepared for a fight. But all the fight, along with half his blood, is drained out of him. "We call first, yes?" he groans. "On our cellular mobiles. We are then let in through a side gate. That gate leads to a door and a vesti...vesti..."

"Vestibule," Georgie interjects on the Russian's behalf.

"Da. Ves-ti-bule. English language is ball-sack hard to learn, yes? Inside Ves-ti-bule, electronic handprint is required."

"Thank God they don't need knee prints," Georgie says. It's a joke. But nobody laughs. Especially the goon.

I reach into his pockets, find his cell. It's an iPhone. Expensive. Rose knows how to treat his Russian employees.

I hand him the phone. "Call! I'm telling, not asking."

Boris uses his thumb to maneuver the touch pad. He thumbs a number contained in his speed-dial list. That's when Georgie presses the barrel of his piece against the back of the goon's head.

"You'd better hope you dialed the correct number and haven't called out your Cossacks," he warns. "Because guess who takes the first bullet?"

"Do not worry," Boris moans. "And you don't know Slavic Cossack from Jewish Cossack."

OK, whatever. But I am worried. Worried he won't make it to the vestibule. We need his handprint or we aren't going to gain access to the fortress. Easy access, anyway.

It's slow going with me acting as a living pair of crutches, but we make our way down the concrete ramp, out the garage.

We maneuver ourselves toward a gate located on the side of the mammoth facility. Truth be told, I'm also concerned about the surveillance cameras Rose has no doubt installed somewhere. To our advantage, however, there are none mounted on the fence. None that are plainly visible, anyway. Makes sense too, for a guy bent on remaining dead in the eyes of the law and the public.

"Side trouser pocket," Boris says at the padlocked gate. "There is key in there, yes?"

Georgie reaches inside for it. He pulls it out. There's blood on it. He wipes the blood off on his pant leg, then inserts the key into the padlock and twists. It opens.

We make our way through the open gate, try for the side door as fast as Boris's moan-and-hobble allows. When we come to the metal door, Boris tells me to take hold of a certain brick that appears to be a part of the normal course work. He points the brick out.

"Pull on it," he insists.

I do it.

An entire brick panel opens, exposing a dimly lit reader screen.

"Do us proud," I say.

When he lacks the strength to raise his hand, I do it for him, pressing his palm against the screen. There's an abrupt mechanical click that signals something releasing, like a lock, and the metal panel door opens by a few inches. Georgie grabs hold of it and opens it wide.

"We'll take it from here," I say to Boris, dragging him inside and releasing him.

He drops down in the corner between the wall and the door, issuing a moan. Georgie applies more tape to his ankles and wrists. Then he asks him, "Where would Rose be right now? His ivory tower?"

Boris just glares at the old pathologist.

"Come on, man," Georgie pushes. "At this point you might as well just tell us."

Boris the Russian goon hawks something slimy up into his throat, spits it out onto the floor. "Mister Rose, he is always up in the tower. Ten floors up. Then another four floors after that."

"What's the easiest way to get up there?" I ask.

"No stairs past floor number ten. Only the freight elevator will take you up from there." He cocks his head in the direction of the elevators. "It is where you'll find dead-or-alive Mister Rose, yes?"

"Someone takes a shot at us, Boris," Georgie warns, "or if this is a setup, we'll come back for you and kill you. Understand?"

"If I am not already dead yet, dude," he says. "Already I am seeing angels."

I'm feeling a little gypped. I don't recall seeing any angels when I died.

Georgie tapes the goon's mouth.

Then we head for the freight elevator.

CHAPTER 47

There's something surreal about the rapid rise in the dark freight elevator. A straight vertical shot up ten stories toward the tower portion of the old Montgomery Ward castle to confront a living Russian spy who's supposed to be dead. There's something very *Batman and Robin* about the experience.

It also seems just a little too easy.

Rose has himself locked away inside a fortress and all it takes is one electronic palm print to get us inside the walls? As if reading my mind, Georgie has his .9 mm out and at the ready. I do the same while the old elevator approaches the top floor.

Until it stops.

The machine just shuts down in between the ninth and tenth floor. There's a disturbing pause that makes my throat close in on itself and my brain buzz from an adrenaline injection. A series of ceiling-mounted bright lights flash on. Lights so bright they blind me. The lights are followed by an incredible noise that screams and vibrates. The noise comes at us like a physical wave. A wall of crushing sound. It rattles the fillings inside my teeth. Both Georgie and I can't help but drop our pieces. We can't help but collapse, incapacitated, to the hard elevator floor, a couple of sad sacks of beat-up bones and flesh.

CHAPTER 48

When the noise finally stops, I lie on the floor of the freight elevator feeling myself go in and out of consciousness. I fight to stay alert, but I know that if the noise sounds again, I'll be out cold. My fragile head won't be able to bear it.

While the blinding white lights continue to shine down on us, the elevator once more starts up. It lifts us up to the one remaining floor. I still can't move. From what I can make out, out the corner of my left eye, neither can Georgie.

When the elevator stops again and the doors slide open, I can't help but raise my head, as painful as the effort is. And what I witness not only empties my lungs of all their breath, it provides the reason Peter Czech tried to blackmail his grandfather.

It all has to do with his severed spine.

CHAPTER 49

Inside a mammoth loft space exists a room constructed inside a room.

The room's walls, ceiling, and floor are created by a thick layer or layers of perfectly translucent plastic held rigid and tight by an intricate stainless-steel framing system. The room is isolated atmospherically with its own ducted HVAC system, which is located right beside it. Placed inside the plastic room's center is an operating table. Surrounding the operating table is a series of bright lamps. Portable monitoring equipment is stacked to the right side of the table, not far out of the way of the half dozen or so people who are standing around the table and the man who's laid out upon it. Face down. A man is filming the operation with a shoulder-mounted video camera, leaning in to get as close to the operating action as he can.

The people are all wearing surgical scrubs. Not the usual hospital pea green scrubs, but white, as if this homespun operating theater were somehow far more special than the usual everyday medical surgery.

And it is. Everyone wears masks, but that doesn't prevent me from recognizing all of them. Or, all the people I should recognize, that is.

As the shock of the noise-subduing system wears off and I somehow collect myself enough to prop myself up onto one knee in the open elevator, I recognize Lola and her half sister, Claudia. The man to their left is someone I've never met before, but whose crazy-assed devil brows I know immediately.

It's Harvey Rose.

The "dead" man issues me the slightest of glances, like Georgie and I are nothing more than the pizza delivery crew, then returns his attention to the operating table action. "Security system spotted you inside the parking garage," he explains in a low, matter-of-fact voice. Then he shouts out, "Boys!"

Two monster goons are on us, dragging us inside the great room. Leaving our automatics where we dropped them on the elevator floor. Just as well—we're a long way from being able to make a fist, much less lift a gun. Behind us, the elevator doors close. The goons pick us up by our jacket collars, and they force us to stand, however wobbly.

Lola peers at me from where she stands by the operating table. Even from a distance of maybe twenty feet, I can see that her brown eyes are glassy, filled with tears. "Richard, why?" she sobs. "Why on God's earth did you come here?"

Before I can answer her, she turns back to the table.

The man doing the operating is being assisted by Claudia. He slams down an instrument. "I cannot work in this way," he grumbles. "Not if you want me to get this right!" He also speaks in a foreign accent. One that isn't Russian, however. More like Spanish.

Rose takes a step back from the operating room table. "Not another word. Anyone!"

I glance at Georgie over my shoulder. He glances back at me.

Behind us stand the goons, ready to pounce on us if we move or speak or fart. In front of me is my longtime lover. On the operating table is a man.

It's Lola's son, Peter Czech.

CHAPTER 50

We're quickly ushered out of the loft and into an empty, windowless room. The room reminds me of a sterile, concrete APD interview room, only without the comfortable amenities. Like a metal ashtray for instance, or those floor-mounted metal rings meant to secure one's shackles. My head is still ringing, and the hardwood floor beneath my feet still feels like mush. But I'm managing to keep it together. More or less.

Georgie doesn't seem to be faring as well. On the surface anyway. He isn't speaking, for one. That has me worried. Usually Georgie can't stop talking. Especially when he's angry, which he surely must be at this point. His face is pale and withdrawn, like that shot of severe noise and blinding white light has more than rattled his brain. Like it's shaken loose his skin cancer, made it spread all throughout his body in a single instant.

The goons tell us to "sit" in their Russian-accented tough-guy voices.

They don't have to tell us twice. Georgie and I drop into the two available metal chairs.

The goons exit out of the room then, close the metal door behind them, and lock it from the outside.

I turn to my big brother. "Can you talk?"

He nods, swallows. "Jesus H," he mumbles, "I think I soiled myself."

I try to laugh. But I can't work up the energy.

"That siren in the elevator," he goes on after a breath-catching beat, "that's one of the newest in army tactical weapons. It can render an entire army defenseless. Yet it leaves them very much alive. Read about in *Pop Sci.*"

"I think my fillings are loose."

"Say a prayer your brain didn't pop, Moon." Pausing to catch his breath. "By all rights, you should be experiencing a stroke-induced coma by now."

"The night is young. Tell me what the fuck *you* think is going on out there and why my girlfriend is involved in it."

"That was Czech on the table. Upside down, damaged spinal column exposed."

"So I noticed."

"Truth revealed. Your man is everything he pretends to be, at least as far as his paralyzed condition goes, Moon. Rose must be putting up the cash for some kind of experimental surgery."

"Why? I mean, why do anything for Czech if he's trying to expose the old man for what he is?"

Georgie sucks in another breath, releases it. I'm wishing he had a medicinal joint on him. His hands are beginning to shake as the pain of his condition settles in.

"If what's being done to him is a surgery that can make him walk again, it might be costing millions of dollars. So you know what I think, Moon? I think Czech issued his old granddad an ultimatum. Put up for the operation or I expose you. Simple as that."

"Why doesn't Rose just kill him instead?"

"Czech is still his grandson, Moon. His blood. Maybe Devil Brows is a softy deep down inside."

"Or maybe Czech has something that Rose wants, and the only way he can get at it is by agreeing to the surgery, keeping him alive."

"PRECISELY, GENTLEMEN!" barks a deep voice from behind us. "Because there's the matter of a flash drive containing thousands of pages of documents and photographs that detail my dealings with the Russian Federation and the former Soviet Union for more than four decades."

I never heard the door open. Never heard Rose walk in, or the two Russian meatheads who stand at the ready behind him.

Georgie and I turn to get a good look at Lola's dad. I notice a distinct resemblance, especially in the eyes, under their wild, now-silver devil brows. Deep, passionate dark pools that don't look at you but look into you and through you. Cut into you.

He moves closer to us, which triggers the meatheads to pull out their weapons—.9 mm Glock automatics. Like Georgie and I are any kind of danger at this point. We're unarmed, still rattled by the siren, and just plain fucking old and worn out.

"Let me guess, Rose," I say. "This the part where you tell us precisely what we want to know since you're going to kill us anyway."

The tall, seventy-something man laughs. His metallic silver eyebrows are so thick and unruly, they curl up at the ends much like a cartoon devil, like the Grinch who stole Christmas.

But he isn't the devil, and he certainly ain't the Grinch.

He's Lola's father, and he's a spy. A traitor. He's somehow managed—most likely with Russian government assistance—to live as a dead man in an era where spy satellites can focus in on how and where you part your hair from three miles up. No wonder he chooses to live a self-induced exile inside this old abandoned white castle. The same building that used to bring me so much happiness as a child but that now makes me sick to my stomach.

"You see, gentlemen," Rose goes on, "it does me no good not to try to give Peter the gift of a healed spine, if the cost of such a miracle is within my means."

"Let me guess," I say. "You didn't always share in that sentiment. Or you wouldn't have ordered me beaten me so badly I actually died for five minutes."

He smiles, like my death is reason for levity.

"I really must apologize for how my men treated you." Glancing over his shoulder at the Russian goons. "My associates are born of a different culture and they sometimes can get carried away. Their orders were to frighten you, not kill you." His eyes back on me. "And as for the operation, I resisted at first because ten million dollars unmarked cash presented a challenge to even a man of my resources."

"Ten million," I repeat. "That's what you're spending on your grandson's back." It's a question.

"For starters," he admits. "And nothing is guaranteed. Not initial surgery, not stem cell injection, not rehabilitation, not follow-up surgeries. Not by a long shot. These doctors were flown in from Brazil. Their English is somewhat limited, but not their skills. They are pioneers at spinal cord surgery, especially for a man like Peter, whose backbone was severed cleanly. He's proving the ideal candidate for surgery and stem cell regeneration. But no one knows if it will last. And, of course, this is all highly illegal in both the eyes of the global medical community and the law."

"Black market stem cells," Georgie mumbles out the corner of his mouth. "Cells lifted from unborn fetuses. No wonder the under-the-table ten million price tag. Christ, they could ask one hundred million and get it."

"You brought Lola into this," I point out. "Far as I'm concerned, Rose, you're a criminal who should be incarcerated in federal prison to serve the first of two or three life sentences. You *and* Peter. I don't care if he's Lola's son, and I don't care if he can't walk."

I hear Georgie clear his throat. "Moon here and I are going to see that you go to the clink, Rose," he states boldly. "How about them rotten fucking apples?"

Good old Georgie. Pain or no pain, he says it like it is.

Rose laughs, runs open hands over his white gown. "You're in no position to be making threats. My friends from back in the former USSR are ready to give you a very, very good spanking whenever I give the order. Your faces will be so swollen and unrecognizable your own mother will pass by you on the street. If you had mothers, I suppose."

The whole if-we-had-mothers dialogue thing tickles the funny bones of the goons at the door. They laugh out loud like Devil Brows Rose is Jay Leno. I feel like a prisoner caught up inside a Bond flick. One of the shitty ones, post-Connery.

"As for Lola," Rose adds, "she cannot help the absolute love she bears for her child. When Peter revealed himself to her some weeks ago, something inside her was freed." He pauses, lowers his hands, stares up at the post-and-beam ceiling. "And something else was revealed to her as well."

"Don't keep us in suspense, Rose." I smile. "Me and Georgie, we're already dead. Am I right?"

"You won't like it, Mr. Moonlight," he says, eyes peering down at the floor. "Especially considering your romantic involvement with my daughter."

I picture myself floating over my body. I once more see my dead body lying in the hospital bed, Lola standing over me. Then I see a young man enter. Some Young Guy who pats her ass while I'm lying dead in the bed. Is that what Rose is talking about? Is that why it will hurt me? The revelation that Lola is seeing someone else?

Movement from beside me.

I turn.

Over my shoulder I see Georgie drop out of his chair. He drops onto his knees. His face turns bed-sheet white, blue eyes bulging, long gray-white hair hanging like a veil. He starts to heave all over the floor. His body trembling and convulsing.

"Someone grab a spoon or a butter knife!" I shout. "Something to open his jaws, stop him from swallowing his tongue or biting it off!"

"Theo!" Rose barks. "Please do something about that vile mess on the floor."

Theo the goon walks out of the room and quickly comes back in with a green towel. He steps over to where Georgie is now foaming at the mouth. He bends at the knees, sets the towel onto the small puddle of bile.

"Mr. Rose, my partner is very sick. He needs medical care. You have to allow your doctor to treat him."

"That doctor is in the middle of experimental spinal cord surgery!" he snaps. "It is not possible."

"Then you have to allow me to take him to a hospital."

Now Rose just laughs. "Really, Mr. Moonlight. Lola has described you as being far more intelligent than that."

It feels strange knowing that my sig other has been talking to this insane man about me.

Georgie is down on his side, curled up in the fetal position.

Theo is down on one knee, trying his best to wipe up the bile, his own face having gone pale, looking like he's about to join Georgie in getting sick. But when Georgie reaches into his side pocket, pulls out his stun gun, and slams it into Theo's neck, the thug chokes and trembles as the electric shock waves neutralize him, sending him face-first down into a puddle of fresh, warm DNA. Courtesy of my big bro and award-winning method actor, Georgie Phillips.

CHAPTER 51

I shoot up, grab Rose by the neck, put a choke hold on him, forearm against Adam's apple. He's taller than me, but far weaker. All skin and bones to which a small round potbelly is attached. The physical makeup of your average paranoid shut-in. He feels like a tall bird in my arm.

The remaining goon draws his piece.

I make like I'm fisting a pistol with my free hand, poke at my forehead with extended index finger.

"Plant your bead, asshole," I insist. "A little above and between the eyes. That's your target. But before your bullet enters my brainpan to join the other one that's in there, I'm gonna snap your boss's neck."

I expect Rose to be trembling in my arms. But he's still and silent. Almost like he *wants* his neck to be snapped. Crap, maybe he does.

"Shoot, Ivan," he demands in a soft, low tone. "Shoot him, and if need be, shoot him through me."

Ivan...

"Ivan?" I repeat. "You serious? Ivan and Theo. Holy crap, this is better than TV."

"Fucker's got a death wish," Georgie says, standing, wiping his mouth with the back of his hand. "You pull that trigger,

Ivan, I will kill you. Just so you know, I got ya covered like a Minute Man missile."

Ivan the Russian goon holds his aim on me. I'm staring down the barrel of a .9 mm. A situation that, sadly, I am all too familiar with.

"Separate," Georgie says.

I begin to drag Rose to one side of the room, and Georgie goes to the other, closing the distance between him and Ivan with each step.

Ivan becomes confused, now shifting his aim from Georgie to me and back to Georgie.

"Do! Not! Move!" he shouts, accent thick, voice wavering, verging on panic.

"Shoot us!" Rose screams.

The gun back on me. The whole thing feels like a fucked-up version of Russian roulette.

Georgie dives, the stun gun held out before him like the tip of a spear.

Ivan's automatic explodes.

Rose goes limp in my arms.

Ivan drops, deadweight, to the floor.

"Get his gun!" I shout.

Georgie snatches it up. How he's able to make himself sick and then move so fast and do it all through waves of full-body pain is beyond me. Survival instinct retained from the jungles of Vietnam maybe, where he was held captive for more than a year by the Vietcong before making his escape.

I lay the deadweight Rose down on the floor.

He's been hit in the lower neck, maybe a half inch away from his carotid artery. The bullet must have taken a nosedive into his lungs because it never exited into me.

"Fuck!" Georgie spits. "Now what?"

Rose is mumbling something. Something about Lola.

"Lola," he's saying. "My...little...girl...Lola. I'm. So. So. Sorry."

The door opens. A man walks in, followed by Lola. I've never met the man before. But I feel like I already know him. And I *do* know him, in a way. The man from my out-of-body experience. The man who came to Lola when I died for five minutes.

He's Some Young Guy.

CHAPTER 52

Lola, dressed in a white smock, sweat-stained white mask hanging down on her chest, the matching white cap still sitting on her head, runs to her injured father. She kneels down over him, takes hold of his hand. She's weeping.

"Get a doctor!" she screams. "One of the surgeons!"

But no one's listening.

The two goons, Ivan and Theo, who've been stung with Georgie's stun gun, are still laid out on the floor, even though both of them have regained enough strength to prop themselves up onto one elbow apiece. But by all indications, the angry Russian bear has been zapped out of them. I can only imagine their regret in not having patted us down before leading us into this room.

Georgie has the .9 mm gripped in his right hand and he's shifting his eyes from me to Lola and Some Young Guy, who stands a few steps inside the doorway. Some Young Guy is the lead man before an entourage of men and women all wearing navy blue Windbreakers, the letters FBI emblazoned upon them in big gold letters.

Entering close behind them, a team of blue-uniformed APD officers, Detective Clyne out in front of them. Clyne and I make eye contact. He nods, his face white and withdrawn, like he hasn't slept in days or been far away from the bottle. Probably both.

I nod back.

Standing beside him is his driver, big Officer Mike.

Mike also purses his lips and nods. Friendly this time, as opposed to the hospital where he flipped me off. I guess my willingness to put myself into the shit all for the cause of right over wrong makes me much more likeable in his eyes. But I'm not so sure if I'm willing to place myself in the shit, so to speak, so much as I possess an uncanny knack for getting myself *into* shit. A head case who's no stranger to shit or train wrecks.

Some Young Guy makes his way to Lola, kneels down beside her. "You need to get back to Peter, Lo," he says. He puts his fingers to Rose's jugular, then looks up at his people. "Not getting a pulse. Need EMTs. Those docs in there can't do this. Call it in now!"

"Already on it, Chief," informs a small woman, who has a cell phone clutched in one hand, her service automatic in the other. As she holsters her weapon, she shoots me a look and a warm smile.

"Thanks," she offers. "For all your help. Any idea how long we've been after Rose and his grandson?"

I turn back to Some Young Guy. He stands up from Rose and takes Lola in his arms. He's her man now, and it makes my stomach drop down around my ankles.

Clyne and his men and the FBI special agents spread out. They remove themselves from the doorway as a team of EMTs burst through and go to work on Rose.

Lola spots me then.

She looks at me while still clutched in the arms of Some Young Guy.

"Oh, Richard," she whispers. "You have no idea, do you?"

"No." I swallow. "You're wrong. I've known for days. When I died, I floated over my body. And I saw you and him, together. I couldn't see his face. But I know it was him."

Lola bears so much sadness in her smile it pains me to look at her.

Standing there with the FBI cuffing the goons, reading them their rights; with sirens blaring outside the building; with God only knows what going on outside that plastic-enclosed operating room; with Rose clinging to life or already dead; with my brain fucked up and my heart breaking, my significant other, Lola, has no other choice but to smile.

Some Young Guy turns to me, approaches. He holds out the hand that isn't holding a hand cannon. "I'm Special Agent Christian Barter. I'm Peter Czech's biological father."

I feel the floor go soft. I'm not going to pass out, but I'm having trouble keeping my balance nonetheless. So what am I supposed to think? Barter sires Lola's kid back when they were teens and goes on to a life of law enforcement? That he just happens to be assigned to Rose's case? Or maybe he pushed to be assigned to it, knowing who Rose was and what he was all about—a devil-browed man who made Lola give up her only child. Whatever Barter's role and how he came to accept it, he's no longer Some Young Guy to me. He's got these wide blue eyes, a mustache, and a goatee sprinkled with gray hairs. He isn't all that young even. But he has a young way about him. Even an optimistic way, despite the circumstances.

"My son is being operated on in the next room." Glancing at Lola over his shoulder. "*Our* son. And right now, with Rose in custody, our son is our priority."

Lola goes to him, takes hold of his hand. "We should go back in."

I watch my girlfriend walk toward the door with the man who fathered her son. Biologically speaking. I can't help but wonder if their bond is one of rekindled love or simply the mutual concern for a son. I choose the latter, but my heart tells me it's the former.

Before they reach the open door, I stop them. "Barter!"

He stops, turns, Lola's hand tightly held in his.

"Are you going to arrest your own son?"

His smile dissolves then, his youthful look of optimism disappearing.

He nods. "If he lives."

CHAPTER 53

Do you know what it's like living every minute like it's your last?

It's not as surreal as you might expect. I'm not afraid. I'm not sad. I'm not paranoid. I grew up surrounded by death as if it were as ordinary as breakfast, lunch, and dinner. You grow up like that, you learn to accept mortality as a normal course in life's grand feast of events. Not something to be ignored or feared. And I live my life like it could end at any minute, that bullet frag shifting inside my brain causing total paralysis and stroke and eventually death.

But I also live my life like I'm going to live forever.

It's not all that different from the way we all live. Because who knows how long we've got. How many times have we heard the story about the man who crossed the road and got hit by a bus? Or the woman who walked into the corner bodega for a Diet Coke and was shot by the guy holding up the store? Or the family that impulsively hopped a flight to Buffalo on a cold winter's night, only for the ill-fated flight to take an unexpected plunge? Or even the middle-aged man who sat down on a calm Sunday afternoon to read a newspaper, fell asleep, and never woke up?

Death happens to all of us. It's always chasing us, and just because you got a better shot at having it happen to you sooner rather than later doesn't make it right for you to skip out on life. And as for me, I want to spend that life in search of the truth, regardless of whether I do right or wrong in the process. As a PI, it's what I do. As a human being, it's what I obsess about.

In this case, I do right.

As Rose's goons are carted away by the APD-accompanied FBI personnel and the near-dead Harvey Rose is rushed to the Albany Medical Center for emergency surgery, I stand beside Georgie, while Barter and Lola stand by their son, whose own surgery is nearly completed.

I could leave the building, my job done, my contract with Czech null and void, my girlfriend lost to the arms of another. But something's keeping me there.

Back to Lola.

It's the way I feel about her—the way my gut feels about her. I haven't confronted her about her conducting an affair these past few days. Not because I'm angry or hurt, but because I'm afraid that if I utter even a single word about it, I'll lose her forever. As the surgeons step away from the table, speak something softly in Portuguese to Lola and Barter, that's precisely what I realize.

The surgeons never do lay their hands upon Peter Czech again.

They abandon the table, shaking their heads in disgust, ripping their sweat-soaked masks from their faces. It's the cue then for the half dozen FBI personnel still hanging around inside the loft to flash their badges at them, explain that they are to be questioned.

My eyes lock on Lola and Barter as they approach their son.

I see Lola take hold of his limp hand. I hear her begin to weep, and then I see Special Agent Barter begin to cry. He wraps his long arm around Lola's shoulder. She's trembling in his arms. Maybe they don't exist as a real family, but at the same time, they are family.

Blood family.

The surgeons are allowed to take their white smocks off and to wash in a makeshift sink that's been set up in a corner beside several fifty-gallon blue medical waste bins. They aren't being arrested or charged as far as I can tell, but they and their cameraman are about to be rounded up and hauled downtown for questioning.

Out the corner of my eye, Detective Clyne is chomping at the bit in the far corner of the loft space, hands stuffed inside the pockets of his trench coat, his eyes shifting from the makeshift surgery to me and back to the surgery again.

I make my way quietly to one of the surgeons. He's a tall, thin man, and his brow is still beaded with sweat.

"Do you speak English?"

He nods.

"The young man you were operating on." I swallow. "How did he die?"

He nods once more, bites his bottom lip, eyes peering at the floor. "Massive coronary. He bore the heart of an alcoholic, despite his tender age. If we had been operating inside a true medical center, he might have lived. But we were not prepared for something like that. Not inside a warehouse. Not with portable equipment." His voice may be heavily accented, but you can't mistake the tone of utter defeat and disappointment sprinkled with fear.

The same small female FBI agent who thanked me before approaches us, takes hold of the surgeon's arm. "That's all for now, Mr. Moonlight," she says. "I'm going to have to ask you and your partner to exit the building along with us. Considering your involvement in this case, I will ask that you follow us to FBI headquarters. Or you can ride with us now."

"I can give you a lift," a man says from behind me. It's Clyne. Not far behind him, his ever-loyal Officer Mike.

I tell them both that I'll take care of carting Georgie and myself downtown. "We'll be right behind you," I assure them.

The agent looks at me, into my eyes. I can tell she's questioning her own judgment by trusting me. She shifts her gaze to Clyne as if to get his blessing.

"He's OK," Clyne says with a nod.

Over his shoulder, I see Officer Mike nod in agreement. Funny how things can change so rapidly.

"Don't worry," I add. "I want to see this thing through as much as you guys do."

"OK then," the special agent says. "See you in a few."

I make my way back over to the operating theater. Lola is still desperately clutching her son, and Barter is still clutching the both of them. You can't help but hear the sobs coming through the heavy plastic. For a brief second I think about going to her. But then I think better of it.

That's when I turn and head for a freight elevator that will take me down. But I'm not entirely sure how much further down I can possibly go.

CHAPTER 54

Georgie and I drive to the FBI headquarters as promised. But not without first making a pit stop at Georgie's townhouse, where we retrieve a much-needed medicinal joint for him and four Advils for me.

The FBI office is in downtown Albany, on lower Broadway, not far from the alley where I took my first beating from Rose's Obama-masked Russian support staff. We're hustled into a glass-walled room that contains that same dark-haired FBI woman, whose name, it turns out, is Lombardi, and Detective Clyne. They've been working with Peter Czech for more than a year, she explains. They were going to arrest him for treason unless he agreed to give them Rose. But in the meantime, he wanted the use of his legs again. That was the deal. If Rose would put up the money, the FBI would agree to allow him the operation.

"But that operation took his life," Lombardi says bitterly. "Now if Rose dies, the entire operation will be in jeopardy and most likely dead too."

"You knew about Czech all along," I point out to Clyne.

The sad cop pulls his hands out of his trench coat pockets, crosses arms over chest. The pursed-lip look on his face is like, *Gotta do what you gotta do, even if it means lying...*

"My apologies," he offers. "I wasn't at liberty to divulge the APD's cooperative efforts in this FBI-led case. My only option was to try to get you to reveal what you knew as an independent working for Czech. But client confidentiality sealed your lips." He smiles a little when he says the thing about sealed lips. Makes him look soft and almost loveable.

"This is a terrifically complicated case, Mr. Moonlight," Lombardi says.

"It goes deeper than just grandfather and grandson?"

"Naturally. We also assumed through the course of your investigation you might end up latching onto some of the other players. Turns out you nearly did."

Georgie sits up in his chair. "Everyone's interested in some sort of zip or flash drive," he offers.

Lombardi steals a glance at her partner. "Do you have any idea where it could be?" she asks, eyes wide. "Be the one thing that would keep this case a case."

"You too, huh?" I say. "Everyone wants that drive. But no one can begin to find it. Least of all me."

The door opens then, and Barter walks in. He looks drained, and there's a small bloodstain on his white button-down shirt. He must have been listening in on the conversation through the one-way glass. He and an entire FBI team, no doubt. He nods at Clyne and Clyne nods back. Then he sits himself down hard in the one remaining chair left inside the square-shaped room.

"OK, Moonlight." He exhales. "I'm sure you have more than a few questions that need answers. Tell you what I'm willing to do. I'm going to give you a chance to ask them right now, right here. You got one shot and one shot only. So let's have at it."

"How long have you known you had a son?" I ask.

"Forever," he answers.

"How long have you known he was working with Rose to sell nuclear secrets to the Russians for cash?"

He blinks at me, like he's weighing how open he should be with me. Gives a tiny nod to himself, like he's decided. "Only this past year, when he contacted me for the first time."

"How long had Lola known that the son she'd given up lived here in Albany?"

"Like me, since last year."

"How long did she know about her father's illegal activities? Her sister?"

"She's always known about him. That he was alive, I mean. She just had no idea that his business was so illegal."

I look at Georgie. He looks back at me. I want to believe that Lola had no idea about her father's business, but my built-in shit detector tells me different.

"Yeah, illegal to the core," I agree. "Selling secrets. Faking his death and living inside an abandoned department store warehouse, all on the former Soviet government's dime."

"Blood and water, pal." He sighs. "Peter is...*was*...her son, and she was determined to protect him."

"I'm not your pal, Barter," I say. Then, "Is Lola going to be indicted too?"

Barter shrugs his shoulders and stands. "Question-and-answer time is about to come to a swift conclusion, Moonlight."

Lombardi's eyes go wide. But Clyne doesn't blink an eyelash.

Barter shoves his hands in his pocket as if to rein himself in, exhales a deep breath. "OK, fair enough," he says, calming himself down. "No, she's not suspected of anything. Truth is, she rarely saw her father. They hadn't spoken in ten years. She also hadn't spoken to her half sister in over ten years. Not until Czech came back into their lives."

"Your son," I say.

He nods. "My son," he whispers, voice cracking.

Silence fills the room like the gas inside a death chamber.

Until Barter breaks the silence once more.

"That's it for now, Moonlight. You and Mr. Phillips can leave. We'll be in touch later on when it's our turn for the questioning." He turns, looks over his shoulder at Clyne. "You good, Detective?"

Clyne purses his lips. "Yeah," he says. "Got nothing to add."

I get up. So does Georgie. We go for the door. I open it. But before I walk out, I have one more question.

"Barter," I say, "do you still love Lola?"

He looks at me, makes hard eye contact, but then looks away with the most defeated expression I've ever seen on one man's face, save Detective Clyne.

It's answer enough.

CHAPTER 55

Georgie and I decide it's time for a drink.

A lot of drinks, bullet in the head be damned. New series of concussions be damned. Concussion-induced blackouts be damned. Spontaneous road boners be...well, you get it.

We head back over to Moonlight's just as the sun is coming up. The bar is locked up and empty, which suits me just fine. Once inside, I uncap two Buds, carry them over to where Georgie is seated. At the same table where I first sat with Peter Czech. Back when he was still alive and I could only assume he had absolutely nothing whatsoever to do with Lola.

I take a long pull on the beer and sit back.

"Answer me a question, Georgie," I say. "Where was Claudia throughout this whole thing? Last I caught sight of her she was assisting the surgeons as a nurse. Not a soul has mentioned a word about her since."

Georgie drinks some beer, cocks his head. "She'll show up. The evil ones always do."

"Or maybe she's halfway to Aruba by now, new identity, a few mil stuffed inside her C-cups. That is, if she can make room."

"But you gotta admit, Moon," Georgie adds, "she is a cutie. A nuclear, black widow kind of cutie."

"Lola is left to pick up the pieces...with Special Agent Some Young Guy."

"Oh cheer up, Moon. At least you've got your health."

He lets out a laugh.

And then the wall behind him explodes.

CHAPTER 56

Georgie and I hit the floor as most of the wall behind us disintegrates into broken boards, shards, and splinters from automatic machine gun fire.

AK-47s.

The unmistakable metallic jingle of 7.62 mm casings spilling onto the hardwood floor like lead confetti. The bar becomes a battleground of exploded rounds, stomped boot heels, and shouts. From down on the floor, face pressed against filthy floorboards, I make out formal orders being shouted out in Russian.

Georgie and I draw our weapons as the entire bar back becomes victim to Russian bullets. Three entire rows of bottles smash and shatter in the rapid gunfire, along with the spraying and spilling of alcohol. That alcohol, what I make most of my money from these days, is now history.

I roll onto my back, plant a bead in the general direction of four black-leather-jacketed men who wear Obama masks, and finger the trigger until the clip empties out. Georgie does the same. But with the lead flying over our heads it's like shooting blind, and we hit nothing.

The shooting stops.

"Lose the weapons," says a fifth person, who's come up on Georgie and me from behind. A small person. Dressed in black like the others. A woman.

Claudia.

She's got her own hand cannon poised on Georgie and me. Must be she slipped out of Rose's castle fortress before the FBI arrived on the scene. She had to know of a secret exit that only she and her father knew about.

Gun in hand, she kneels down beside me and Georgie. She grabs hold of my pistol, tosses it aside. She does the same with Georgie's gun. She holds out her free hand, palm up.

"The zip drive, Mr. Moonlight," she says calmly. "My father is no longer in need of it, and you see, these men very much are."

One of the masked Obamas approaches, kicks both our pistols out of reach with his jackboot.

"Who are they, Claudia?" I ask. "Russian mobsters, am I right? Mafia? Former regular army conscripts?"

"Let's just say they are...or *were*...my dad's partners. Now that he's dead, they require the information that's on that zip drive. It's worth an unbelievable amount of money to the right buyer, and should it get into the wrong hands..." She allows the notion to drift, its message more than obvious.

So that's it, then. Rose never made it. He must have been DOA by the time he got to the Albany Medical Center. Or she's lying. Not that either scenario matters at this point. Now that he's gone, Claudia is working the Russians, trying to gain their loyalty when they clearly want to form their own camp now that the big boss is dead. Long live the boss.

"No prison for you, am I right, Claudia?"

"Life in a concrete cell surrounded by lesbians does not appeal to me." She smiles. "I'm only twenty-eight years old, and I most definitely prefer cock to pussy."

When she kneels down, I can't help but get a look at her substantial cleavage, like now's the time for love.

Georgie must notice me noticing. "For Christ's sake, Moon," he says.

"Right, Georgie," I say, sitting up. "I'm in control." Then to Claudia. "Mind if I stand?"

The Obama facing down upon me keeps on poking me with his AK. It's fucking annoying, so I reach up, push the black barrel away. He shifts the weapon, presses the stock into his shoulder, plants a point-blank bead on my head.

"Go ahead and shoot, asshole," I tell him. "I could buy the farm at any time."

"Back off," Claudia orders the Russian. "Mr. Moonlight is about to provide us with what we came for." Then smiling at me. Sexy. Enticing. "It's not Christmas yet, but you're in a giving mood, aren't you, Mr. Moonlight?"

I stand up, brush myself off.

Georgie stands too.

Claudia holds out her hand, and with a quick Rita Hayworth shake of her head, repositions her long, lush blond hair. For a brief moment, I consider being her slave.

"The flash drive, please."

I shake my head. "Ain't got it," I reveal.

The Obama raises up his AK again, pulls back the bolt.

"I'm not playing, Moonlight!" Claudia barks. "Time is of the essence now that the FBI is involved. We know you have it because we know Czech personally handed it to you."

"He doesn't remember," Georgie snarls. "You see, he's got this problem with his head."

"Of course," Claudia says, "there's a bullet in his brain. Mr. Moonlight is a rare human being. A suicide who survived a gunshot to the brainpan. Well, now he can very much have his suicide once he gets us the zip drive. Or perhaps we should just execute you now, then scour the place for it. In the end we'll burn the bar with you in it. Yes, come to think of it, that's what we're going to do."

Claudia takes a step back.

"Execute them!" she shouts. "Blow their fucking brains out, then rip the joint apart and don't stop until you find the flash drive."

The Obama in front of me presses the barrel of the AK into my stomach, pushes me back up against what's left of the wood wall. Georgie stands back along with me.

The other three men all take a step forward, aiming their AKs at Georgie and me. The stomach-poking Russian steps back and joins them to create a formal firing squad.

"Are you sure this is what you want, Mr. Moonlight?" Claudia poses.

"I told you," I say. "I have no idea about a zip or flash drive."

She steps back. "On three, gentlemen."

"Wait!" Georgie shouts. "I want a cigarette. If I'm going to fucking take a bullet, I want a cigarette. OK? I get that much, especially 'cause...'cause...'cause *he* dragged me into this."

I turn to my big brother, give him a look like, *Are you for real?* "Way to stick by me in our mutual time of need. Blaming me? I didn't put a gun to your head when I asked you to help—"

"Shut the fuck up, Moon. You really are a fuckup, you know that? A never-ending train wreck, no matter who's on board with you. Holy shit, dude. Just give these people the flash drive! Who cares what's on it or what they're going to do with it. Just hand it over. You think holding back isn't going to get us killed in the end anyway? Is holding back going to change the way of the world? You think that by *not* having the flash drive in their possession they *won't* be able to sell rogue Soviet-era nuclear warheads to Iran or the Taliban? Or maybe you think that what's on it will result in Times Square getting nuked, or Israel getting blown into the Stone Age. Listen, Moon, my half-a-brain friend, who fucking gives a fuck! I don't care, and nor did I care back when Nixon sent me to die fighting the Soviet-backed commies in Vietnam. So if I'm gonna die now all because of you and your silly morals or values, I want to smoke my way out."

Claudia smiles. I think she really likes Georgie. "A cigarette for my very short-lived friend, George," she orders.

The closest of the four masked Russians reaches into the interior pocket of his leather jacket, produces a pack of Marlboro Reds, shakes one out. He pops it into his mouth, lights it himself with a Zippo, then pulls the lit butt out, hands it to Claudia. She in turn gently places the cig between Georgie's lips.

"How about you, Mr. Moonlight?" she kindly offers. "One final smoke?"

"No, thanks," I lie. "Those things will kill you. 'Sides, Marlboro Reds ain't my brand."

"Fuck him," Georgie says, pulling on the cig. "If it were me…if I knew where the hell the flash drive was…I'd give it to you. You should consider that right now, maybe. Or is it that now I got no choice but to die for him? In any case, I say he doesn't get a final smoke. No way, José. Sayonara, motherfucker."

The Russian gunmen laugh at that. Georgie's words must remind them of a Schwarzenegger action flick, because the

Russian farthest to the right turns to the one on his left and says, "Hasta la vista, motherfucker," in a deep, faux-Austrian-accented voice mixed with real Russian-slash-English.

The third one down turns to him, shakes his head. "You of course have it fucking wrong, yes? It is 'Yippee ki-yay, mother-fucker.' And it is Bruce Willis, yes?"

"Hasta luego," the first man corrects himself. "Arnold Schwarzee-nazi!"

They all get a kick out of that one.

"Hasta la vista, baby," corrects the second one in. "That is from Schwarzenegger." Then he starts rattling the shit off in his own version of the Schwarzenegger monotone: " 'I'll be back!' 'Consider this a divorce!' 'If it bleeds we kill it!' 'Say hello to my little friend.' "

"No, stupid fucking asshole," chimes in the first one. "That will be Al Pacino. *Scarface*. Bad-ass *Scarface*, yes? You don't fuck with *Scarface*, stupid asshole. Even the colored people don't fuck with *Scarface*."

Claudia turns to us. "See the shit I put up with?" she says, shaking her head. "Too bad you two chose the wrong side. You'd make wonderful employees." Then, looking down at her wristwatch. "You almost done, George?"

But Georgie isn't listening. He's smoking and doing something strange for the hard-assed Vietnam vet. He's crying. Real tears stream down his face.

Claudia takes a step forward. "Don't cry, George," she consoles. "We all owe God a life. Your time to pay the big guy has just come, that's all."

He nods, pulls the cig from his lips, stares down at the lit end, grabs a fistful of Claudia's left breast, tosses the cig into the spilled alcohol, and hits the floor with her.

The fire plumes up into a red-orange haze just as I go down onto my belly.

The Chatty Cathy Russians start blasting in all directions. Georgie reaches into Claudia's jacket, finds her piece, plants the barrel on the four goons, and empties the clip into their legs. They drop like iron curtains as the fire spreads to the walls of the bar and up into the ceiling. Flames roar, but the shooting stops.

Just then we hear the sirens from the squad cars and vans that surround the bar's exterior. The back door explodes open. An army of feds and APD spill into the burning gin mill.

"Out now!" screams Special Agent Barter. Clyne is standing directly beside him, his service weapon drawn.

We don't argue.

Georgie lets go of Claudia as Barter grabs hold of her jacket, pulls her out the back door. It's then, as I'm getting up from the floor, in the glare of the spreading flames, that I see it. Stuck to the underside of the overturned table. The flash drive.

The flash drive is stuck to the underside of the table by a big piece of chewing gum. Czech must have planted it there back when he first came to see me a little more than a week ago. He knew that the table was my table alone and that no one else was allowed to sit at it. He knew the drive would be safe there, plastered to the bottom via an old chewed-up piece of Juicy Fruit. As the fire approaches me like foaming, lapping waves, I pull the flash drive from the table and make a run for the back door.

I'm not outside for more than five seconds before the fire flashes and the bar roof collapses.

Moonlight's Moonlit Manor falls.

CHAPTER 57

As usual, I'm out of a job.

So are the Russian Obamas, who are pulled out of the fire just in time before their Latex masks melt to their faces. In any case, they'll be spending considerable time in the hospital nursing their leg wounds. And after that, I foresee prison time in a maximum-security federal penitentiary. I also know that eventually they'll be extradited back to their homeland, where they'll probably co-host a prime-time cable television reality show. Welcome to the new, post-Communist Russia.

We stand in a circle, feeling the heat of the fire on our faces, with EMT-provided towels covering our shoulders. Me, Georgie, Agent Barter, Clyne, and several FBI agents, including Special Agent Lombardi. For a time we all look on like happy campers at a bonfire as the firemen hopelessly stand around the still-burning remains of Moonlight's.

"Don't suppose you took out an insurance policy on the joint," Georgie says after a time.

I cock my head. "You need cash for that."

He smiles.

Barter shoots me a glance. He still seems very sad.

"How's Lola?" I ask.

"Lost her son *and* her old man today," he says and exhales. "Not great. But she's strong. I forgot just how strong she was until we came back into one another's life."

His words lodge themselves inside my stomach like so many stones. He's done his share of crying today too. For a son he never got the chance to know. A son he would have been forced to arrest had he lived. But also a son who might have been spared a life sentence due to his willingness to cooperate with the law. I can't imagine the internal conflict Barter's experiencing right about now.

"Take care of Lola for me, will you?"

He exhales. Then, "Did you really see me inside that hospital room? When you died for a few minutes?"

I nod. "It's the truth."

The corner of his mouth rises up just enough to offer the hint of a smile. "So maybe there's something to the afterlife thing, after all," he says.

Takes me a beat, but I see what he's getting at. His dead son somehow having a life beyond the earthly life.

"You can count on it, Barter," I offer. What the hell else can I say to him?

He holds out his hand for me. I look down upon it for a moment, but then I take it in mine and give it a squeeze. He starts to say something as he gently pulls his hand away, but in the end, he just closes his mouth and shakes his head. It looks like his chin is about to drag on the ground when he walks away from me toward his ride.

I pull off the towel, toss it back to one of the EMTs.

Georgie does the same. "Think one of your people can give us a lift home?" he asks Agent Lombardi. "Assuming you wanna impound my bloody Beetle."

"I'm on it," she smiles warmly. A little too warmly. Together, she and Georgie start walking like they're about to head out on their first date together. Fucking Georgie. "Coming, Moon?" he asks over his shoulder.

"Be there in a minute," I say.

But as they walk away, I see someone coming up on me from over my left shoulder. At first I can't help but think it's my old man. But that's impossible because he's dead. As the four-by-four of a man approaches through the haze of the fire and the black smoke emerging from it, I see that it's Uncle Leo, my most loyal customer.

"We're closed, Uncle Leo," I say. It's a joke. He doesn't laugh.

He comes close, looks up at me with his always-teary eyes. "Did you save it?" he says, voice gravelly with worry, his still-thick head of gray hair slicked back against his skull with Brylcreem.

"I'm not reading you, Uncle Leo," I say, suspecting that he's already tipped a few beers at home. But when he motions with his hands for me to lean down in close to him, I don't smell even a hint of booze on his breath.

He brings his lips close to my ear. "The box," he says. "Did you save the computer box?"

I stand upright. "How..." It's all I can get out.

"That nice young fella in the wheelchair," he offers. "He waited for me that night, when he came in to see you. He waited inside his car for me. He called me over and he told me that he stuck a small plastic computer thingamajig to the underside of your private table. He said it was very important—that it contained secrets that those goddamned Russian commies want. It was up to him to find a place to hide it where no one would think of looking for it. So that's when he thought about sticking it under your table, for just a few days. He paid me two thousand dollars cash to keep an eye on it, from morning till night, so long as you were open. He said you knew all about the plan, but that I was forbidden to talk with you about it." He laughs suddenly, his voice mixing with burning timbers. "Made me feel pretty damned good to be fighting the war again, even from a barstool. And when you closed up early a couple of times, I nearly worried my seventy-nine-year-old ass off that come morning, the computer box would be gone."

I find myself nodding. Because all this time, my one and only, perpetually buzzed client knew of the exact location of that flash drive. The box that cost me considerable pain and even my life. So, just like Uncle Leo, I begin to laugh. Laugh out loud. Laugh so hard the firemen and APD and local TV reporters milling about the scene start shooting us glances.

"Sorry about your bar, Uncle Leo," I say, finally. "We'll have to find you a new one." Then I reach into my pocket and produce the flash drive in the palm of my hand. "And don't worry. Job well done. Our secret computer thingamajig is perfectly safe. And so is the United States of America." Holding my hand up to my forehead in military salute fashion. "Uncle Leo, you have fought your final battle in the war against communist aggression. You are hereby relieved of duty."

He reflexively goes to return the salute, then settles for patting me on the back. "Jeez, Moonlight, there's spies all over the goddamned place," he warns. "No saluting. And that computer thingy, take good care of it. The entire freedom-loving world depends on the information stored inside it, however the hell they're able to stuff it all in there."

"Aye, aye, Uncle Leo," I assure him. "I'll guard it with my life."

He turns then, takes one last look at the fire, and starts walking the opposite way, back across the rear parking lot toward his home. "I'll be drinking at the house from now on, case you need me," he mutters. "I'll be with the wife. She has no idea how much James Bond and I have in common."

The swagger in his walk is unmistakable as he leaves the scene of my burning bar.

CHAPTER 58

Which leaves me pretty much alone to face Detective Clyne.

I hold the flash drive up for him so he can see it.

"I thought about handing this over to the feds," I say. "But somehow giving it to you seems better. Besides, you might use this as leverage over the course of your investigation. My experience is that the feds can be pretty bossy. They suspect you're in possession of the flash drive, they might buy you lunch now and again. Or even a cocktail." But what I'm not telling him is that I'd rather my girlfriend's new boyfriend be denied the holy grail of their investigation. Just because.

I toss it to him.

He snatches it out of the smoky midair. Takes a reflective moment to gaze upon the small device resting in the palm of his hand.

"This *is* the investigation," he offers with a nod. "Fifty years' worth of documents, letters, photos, rogue warhead locations, nuclear sub specs, prices, names of sellers, names of buyers, transactions, Swiss bank account numbers, safety deposit box locations, cash drops..." He stares down at the drive and smiles, even giggles. "Jesus, it's all in here. This thing's worth more than Fort fucking Knox." Cocking his head. "To the right buyer, of course."

I'm staring at the drive too. "Proves Rose was selling secrets to the Russians too, I imagine. First as a federal government accountant employed by the Department of Military Affairs, and later through his grandson, a nuclear engineer in the employ of the Knolls atomic plant in Schenectady."

"That it does," Clyne says, looking off into what's left of the fire. Together, we watch the remainder of the building cave in slowly, like a dying, gut-shot deer collapsing under its own weight. "Peter Czech was a traitor," he says, "and one hell of an optimist. Hired you, thinking you'd keep his flash drive safe while you exposed his grandfather, all while he went to work regaining the use of his legs. And when all was said and done, he'd use the flash drive and the evidence you gathered up against Grandpa Rose as his get-out-of-jail-free card."

"I guess that about sums up the grand plan," I say. "But sometimes optimism isn't enough, is it? In the end the bastards still find a way to nail you to the cross."

I shoot a glance at the cop's left hand. At the ringless finger.

"You miss her, don't you, Clyne? Even though she was unfaithful."

He turns to me, nods.

"Yeah," he says, above the crackling noise of the fire. "Even though she was unfaithful."

I remember Barter standing beside Lola in my hospital room. Her old lover drawn to her side to console her in her grief on the day I died. Turns out he'll be consoling her again. But not over me...my life *or* my death. He'll be consoling her over the death of their own flesh and blood.

"I know exactly how you feel," I say.

He lets out another small laugh. "Do you?" he says, once more staring down at the flash drive.

I don't know how to answer that one. Because maybe I truly have no idea how he feels about being cheated by the one person he must have loved more than himself. No idea, other than he's suffering from the pangs of a broken heart. And who hasn't suffered one of those before?

Tossing the drive up into the air like he's flipping a coin, he catches it again with the same hand. Then he shoves it into the pocket of his trench coat.

"All's well that ends well, or not so well," he says. "Gotta get this thing tagged and bagged and stored away safely in evidence." Tossing me another teddy bear smile, he adds, "I'll be seeing you, Moonlight."

"Sure thing," I say, but as I watch the brokenhearted detective walk away from the smoldering remnants of Moonlight's, my built-in shit detector pokes me against my ribs and speaks up loud and clear.

It says, *You might never see Detective Clyne again.*

CHAPTER 59

He disappears, of course.

A week after Moonlight's burns to the ground and the flash drive that proves Rose and his grandson Peter Czech are traitors is discovered stuck to the underside of my own barroom table, APD Officer Dennis Clyne is declared officially missing and wanted by the FBI for absconding with evidence crucial to a federal and state investigation, or whatever the official term for it is.

But in unofficial terms, Clyne is wanted for turning traitor and for disappearing from US soil with the intention, no doubt, of selling the flash drive to the highest bidder on the black market.

So in the end, it's Clyne who gets his face plastered up on the wall of every post office from Portland, Maine, to Portland, Oregon. I have to admit, I can't help but picture the stocky, sad-faced man sitting inside a café, maybe in Paris. Drinking a solitary coffee, staring out at no one in particular but remembering the wife he loved and lost so painfully to another man.

Maybe he has every intention of selling the flash drive, or maybe he'll hold on to it for a while. Just long enough for the feds to give up on finding him and for Interpol to toss in the towel.

I haven't known Clyne for very long, or at all well, for that matter. But what I do know of him tells me that he's a pretty smart cookie, and that if he has any flaw at all it's being sensitive enough to agree to leave his job in the Bronx to raise a family up here in the country, as it were.

Albany.

I imagine him losing some weight, maybe shaving his head, growing a beard that he'll keep trimmed. He'll dress in black and perhaps take up smoking. He'll blend in with the surroundings, maybe refer to himself as an artist at work, or something like that. He'll have access to those Swiss accounts and secret cash drops, and once he unloads that flash drive he'll have more cash than he ever dreamed about. Certainly enough to pay for a new identity, a new passport, a new soul altogether.

Maybe he'll even be able to afford a black-market cadaver that he'll then arrange to have dropped into the Seine and fished out by the police, who will then have no choice but to declare APD Detective Dennis Clyne dead. Only then will his investigation be called off. Only then will Clyne declare himself the ultimate winner in the matter of Harvey Rose and Peter Czech and one very wayward wife.

But he'll be wrong.

Dead wrong.

He won't be the winner. Because I doubt that, as the years pass, he'll ever truly know happiness again. No matter how hard he works at his new identity and his new home, he'll always be left with the heartache of knowing his wife was bedding down with another man. And the bitterness in that pill never goes away.

Still, I can't help but be happy for Clyne.

Maybe I'm a little envious, even.

Who doesn't wish, from time to time, that he could escape his life and become somebody else? Who doesn't sometimes wish to flee his broken heart? Who can ever truly blame a brokenhearted man for wanting to disappear?

So as the night gives way to the early-morning hours on the day after Detective Dennis Clyne of the APD is declared wanted by the FBI, I get undressed and slip under the covers of my bed alone, and I contemplate those very questions. Who hasn't imagined himself escaping from it all at one time or another? Who hasn't thought about disappearing at least once in his lifetime?

As I begin to drift away, I see Lola, and I feel my heart ache. I see her tan face, her deep-set eyes, and her long thick hair draping her shoulders. I can even smell her lavender scent.

I wonder if I'll be able to live without her. I wonder if I'll ever get over the pain of her leaving me for her old lover, the father of the son she never got a chance to love like a mother. I wonder if I'm the true loser in all of this, and somehow Barter the absolute winner-take-all, even if he has lost his son in the process. I wonder if, in the final analysis, that's the underhanded reason behind Czech hiring me: to expose Lola's affair with the man who should have been his father, to bring them into the light so they could be together. Or maybe I'm just a fool for thinking so. A train wreck of a head case.

But I also can't help but wonder, as a whiskey-infused sleep takes over and my soul begins to slip away, if I'll ever get Lola back. My Lola. I wonder if she'll ever need me again. If she'll ever want me. Desire me. Trust me. And if she does, I wonder if I'll want her again. Wonder if I can trust her. Or if our love is just too badly broken and beyond repair.

Inevitably, we are all dead men and dead women. But until that time comes, we all become the victims of love, slaves to our most painful memories, jesters to our desires.

Maybe I'm just better off dead and buried.

I might drift off to the wetness of my tears dropping onto the pillow one by bloody one. But tonight, as darkness consumes me and all consciousness flees my fragile brain, I begin to sleep the sleep of the dead.

And I cry for no one.

TO BE CONTINUED...

ACKNOWLEDGMENTS

I didn't get here all by myself. I had help. Lots of it. Especially from Chip MacGregor, the one agent who was able to set my career back on the right track. I of course owe a huge thanks to the Thomas & Mercer family, including editors Andy Bartlett and David Downing. Also a shout-out to Jacque and Rory. Thank you to some fellow authors and small-press publishers who offered their support and time along the way, including Dave Zeltserman, Les Edgerton, Chris Barter, Aaron Patterson, Bri Clark, Erica Crockett, Rebecca Logan Holdsworth, Belinda Frisch, Rebecca Buckley (who kicked off the Moonlight series), and all those who are never far from my thoughts. Last but never least, a special hug and kiss to the real-life Lola. We weren't always together, but then we were never really apart.

ABOUT THE AUTHOR

Photograph by Laura Roth, 2012

Vincent Zandri is the best-selling author of *The Innocent, Godchild, The Remains, Moonlight Falls, The Concrete Pearl, Scream Catcher,* and the forthcoming *Murder by Moonlight.* He received his MFA in writing from Vermont College, and his work has been translated into several languages. An adventurer, foreign correspondent, and freelance photojournalist for RT, Globalspec, and IBTimes, among others, Zandri lives in New York.